Daryas

A Vanguard Origin

Written By:

R.D. Wolfe

● Table of Contents

Chapter I – Ash and Bone

The air reeked of rot and burning plastic.

It clawed at Daryas' lungs as she ducked into the storage chamber; the door groaning shut behind her. Her mother's hand pressed firm against her back, guiding her between crates of sealed rations and decommissioned radio parts, toward the narrow crawl space at the rear of the bunker.

"Down. Don't speak," her mother whispered, voice clipped, already turning back toward the entrance. "Stay here. No matter what you hear."

Daryas obeyed. Six years old, knees on concrete, heartbeat pulsing behind her ears.

Above them, something crashed—a hollow metal thump, then another. Screams filtered through layers of rebar and plating, too far to make out the words, but not far enough to forget the sound. The undead were inside the walls.

She crouched lower. The floor was cold, grit biting into her palms where she braced herself. A half-eaten protein bar lay near the edge of the crawl space, the wrapper half-torn and stained with something dark. It smelled faintly sweet—stale apples and iron. She turned her face away.

Her mother's boots creaked once on the steel grate outside the crawl space. Then silence.

Daryas stayed where she was.

She didn't move when the shouting stopped. Didn't breathe when the first body hit the bunker wall. She waited. Eyes wide open, fingers trembling against the floor.

When the handle finally turned and the door creaked open again, she knew by the way the footsteps landed—heavy, uneven—that it wasn't her mother coming back.

The boots stopped just short of the crates.

Daryas held her breath. Her cheek pressed against the floor now, the cool concrete leeching warmth from her skin. Through a gap in the slats, she saw a smear of black oil—or blood, maybe—dragged in from outside. The scent was stronger now. Copper, mildew, and something older. Something dead.

The footsteps moved again. Slow. Pausing between each step like they were listening for something. She clamped a hand over her mouth.

There was a wet shuffle, the sound of weight dragging behind bare feet. No gear. No voice. Whatever had come in didn't need to speak.

She counted the breaths between each movement. One. Two. Hold. Three. Four.

Something knocked over a canteen. It clattered to the ground and rolled until it hit a crate—then silence again.

Daryas didn't cry. She didn't even blink. She lay motionless while something rotten wandered only feet away from her hiding spot. And when the thing finally staggered back through the door—when the bunker groaned shut again and silence took hold like a blanket—she stayed where she was.

She didn't know how long she waited. Could've been minutes. Could've been an hour.

Eventually, the silence changed.

A knock.

Three soft raps—metal on metal. Her mother's signal.

She crawled out slowly, cautious. Her knees were stiff, her palms scraped raw. The room smelled worse now—something had leaked near the door, dark and thick, like boiled meat left out too long.

She reached the door and opened it.

Her mother stood there, blood on her shoulder, the rifle in one hand and a fire axe in the other. Her jaw was clenched tight. Her other arm hung limp, useless. But she was alive.

"You didn't move," her mother said, voice low. A whisper full of smoke. "Good."

Daryas looked at the wound but didn't speak.

Her mother knelt, eyes level with hers. "I don't know if we're getting out of this stronghold. But you did what you were told. You survived." A breath. Then, "Come on. There's an opening for us."

They crossed the perimeter just before first light, what was left of it. The fence had been torn down in places, the heavy stanchions bent inward like something had pressed from every angle at once. Beyond that, there was nothing but open frost and broken scrub, the kind of terrain that offered no cover and no comfort—only questions about who had come through before and whether they'd made it farther than this.

Daryas moved quietly between her parents, her pack slung awkwardly over both shoulders, rubbing at the raw spot on her collarbone with every shift. Her father led the way, his steps light but sure, a long, matte-black rifle resting across his chest. A soft pink hue pulsed from the barrel's power core, barely noticeable under the rising gloom. But in darkness, even the faintest glow became a beacon.

He'd wrapped the core in cloth—a layered mesh from an old supply tent, stitched with heat-resistant threading—but it didn't mask the light entirely. Every so often, he would stop, crouch behind cover, and unwrap the weapon just enough to check the charge. The moment the casing came off, the glow would pulse against the snow-covered brush, casting shadows in every direction like an exposed wound.

Her father didn't talk about the weapon. Didn't explain where it came from, or how he'd gotten in. But he checked it constantly, like it was the one thing he could still control. Daryas had seen him aim it only once, just before they escaped the breach. The recoil had knocked dust from the rafters and snapped the spine of whatever thing had gotten too close. She hadn't seen its face. She didn't need to.

They traveled by night and buried themselves during the day—beneath brush piles, inside fractured culverts, wherever the land dipped low enough to hide them. Sleep came in short, fitful stretches. The cold soaked into their joints. Her mother whispered stories sometimes, old ones, about river towns and greenhouses and places where you could sleep with both boots off.

Daryas never asked where those places were now. She suspected her mother didn't know either.

On the fifth night—maybe sixth—they found a break in the valley that ran sharp and narrow, pinched between rock walls streaked with old soot. A fire had rolled through here once. Nothing but blackened trees and ash-covered roots remained. The air smelled scorched even now, years later, like the valley had learned to carry memory in its bones.

Her father paused just inside the narrow pass and turned slowly, scanning the ridgeline. "Too quiet," he muttered.

Her mother stepped forward, voice low. "Wind's blowing wrong. Can't smell anything."

Daryas stayed between them, her boots crunching over frost-laced dirt. The world didn't feel dead. It felt waiting. Like the silence was watching.

When they reached a bend in the pass, they saw the signs.

A broken thermal sheet, flapping from a low tree limb. Bones in the snow—mostly small, charred black. Bullet casings glinting pink in the moonlight. Not standard-issue. Raiders had been here, and recently.

Her father dropped to a crouch, pulling the cloth from his rifle just enough to check the core. The pink glow lit the edge of his face, catching the hard line of his jaw, the scar near his temple she'd never had the courage to ask about. He wrapped it quickly, then motioned to the slope beyond.

"We move fast," he said, glancing once at Daryas, then to her mother. "We get out of this channel before sunup."

They pushed higher into the ridge, keeping low. Daryas moved quietly, focusing on her footing, her weight, the rhythm of her breath. Her mother had told her once that noise was the first thing to die in a fight—whoever lost control of their noise usually lost everything else right after.

They heard the first voice just as they reached the ridge crest.

Low. Tense. Not panicked—commanding.

Daryas dropped to the ground beside her mother, who pulled her close with one arm and peered over the edge. Her father had already flanked left, disappearing into the shadows with the rifle held low. The pink glow was hidden now, but the silence around it felt taut, like a drawn wire.

Below, three figures stood near a collapsed storage crate, the remnants of someone else's outpost scattered around them. One was holding a torch—not a trexium flare, just firelight, flickering and crude. It cast long shadows across their faces, but Daryas could see the weapons. Long-barrel rifles. Scrap-plate armor sewn into the sleeves of heavy jackets. Not soldiers. Not scavengers. Raiders, clearly marked by their lack of insignia and their readiness to shoot anyone who asked what they were doing there.

Her mother didn't speak, didn't move. Only squeezed her shoulder once, a silent warning.

Daryas didn't breathe.

Her father returned ten minutes later, motioned to circle east. No confrontation. Not tonight.

They moved for hours, arcing wide around the group and into the next hollow. Her father never unwrapped the rifle again, not until they'd put three ridgelines between them and the firelight. Even then, he only checked it once, quietly, before covering it again.

Daryas didn't sleep that morning. Her hands were too cold, her mind too full. She watched her mother build a blind out of dry branches and frost-caked vines, watched her father dig a shallow divot in the snow where they could lie low and vanish from the world.

She curled up in the hollow beside them, eyes fixed on the horizon where the sun tried and failed to break through the ash-streaked clouds.

She didn't ask what came next. She just continued walking with her parents, doing her best not to let her smaller stride slow them down or let her fall behind.

She didn't know how many steps it would take to make the fear that she felt so consistently go quiet, but she planned to count them anyway.

Chapter 2 – Of Futures to Come

The walls in this one didn't creak when the wind shifted, and that was the first thing Daryas noticed. At night, while her father bolted their cot frame to the floor and her mother strung blackout fabric across the seams in the outer paneling, she rested her hand on the support beam just above the heater line, listening to the hum that traveled faintly through the steel. It wasn't the usual cough of overworked generators or the high drone of bad wiring. It was steady, even—like something in this place had been built correctly and, for once, left alone long enough to hold.

She didn't ask how many moves had passed. Twelve, maybe thirteen. The last few blurred together, one relocation folding into the next with the same urgency—take what you can carry, load fast, move before they find you. There wasn't room for nostalgia, only repetition. The days weren't counted by seasons anymore, but by how many times they'd torn everything down and rebuilt it somewhere new. This stronghold was just another shape in the cycle, but it felt different in ways she couldn't quite explain. The corridors were better lit. The outer perimeter checks actually came back with full teams. And now and then, she'd catch a glimpse of someone she remembered from two or three moves ago, someone she thought hadn't made it, sharing a meal with the same hollow-eyed steadiness they all wore now.

In the central corridor, just past the mess prep unit, Daryas shifted crates of worn-out field gear, separating pieces that could be patched from those headed to scrap. The sleeves were stiff with salt from old sweat, the shoulder pads frayed from repeated use. One of the jackets bore the outline of a bloodstain, dried and faded, but unmistakable. She didn't dwell on it. She folded the jacket with the same care as the others and laid it into the repair pile.

The low chatter of soldiers returning from night patrol filtered through the half-open hatch behind her. Their boots scraped against the mesh flooring, voices tired but controlled, carrying the clipped cadence of people who knew better than to relax fully, even behind walls.

She heard one of them say something about a beacon that had gone dark again. The words came muffled—sector numbers, last pings, possible drift. Maybe a relay fry. Maybe something worse. No one said it outright, but the undercurrent in their tone was clear enough. Comms were failing more often. Not in big, dramatic ways—just little failures, small silences. And in this world, silence always meant something.

She didn't stop working. The knife in her hand slipped easily through the strap bindings as she trimmed away the shredded ends. The edges of her fingers were raw, but she welcomed the sensation. It gave her something tangible to focus on.

The door creaked, and someone leaned into the frame.

"You eat yet?"

PK. He held a coil of cable under one arm and a ration bar in the other, the foil wrapper reflecting the low hallway lights as he tilted it toward her. His sleeves were rolled, his forearms marked with shallow weld scars and the dirt that never really washed out of utility fabrics. He didn't wait for her answer. He tossed the bar lightly, and she caught it without looking up.

"You miss another meal, and I'm getting blamed when you pass out mid-shift," he said, not unkindly.

Daryas tucked the bar into her jacket pocket and kept folding gear. "I don't pass out."

"Sure," PK replied, letting the moment sit between them without any teasing. He glanced at the stack beside her. "You did all these?"

She gave a slight nod.

"Not bad," he said. "You ever think about working full-time in gear?"

"I'm not old enough."

"Doesn't matter. Sam says you move quieter than half the new recruits."

She didn't respond, though her hands paused for just a breath before reaching for the next jacket. That Sam had said something like that meant more than she was willing to admit. She had never spoken much to him, but he noticed things. He'd been the one to adjust her boot straps two moves ago when hers had worn through and no one had any in her size.

PK didn't press. He stepped back into the hall, gave the doorframe a single tap with his knuckle as he left, and disappeared down the corridor.

Daryas stayed behind, sorting through the last of the gear until her hands stopped shaking.

Later, after curfew but before lights-out, she lay on the cot with the blanket pulled up to her chin. Her father was already asleep in the bunk across from hers, one arm draped loosely over the edge, the other curled toward his side in a position he never seemed to shift from. She waited until his breathing slowed— deep and even—and slid off her cot onto the cold floor.

The chill bit at her knees as she crouched beside the bed frame. She knew where to reach. The bottom drawer didn't lock. It stuck slightly, the panel warped from old water damage, but she knew the angle to pull without making noise.

The cloth-wrapped rifle was still there, tucked beneath a blanket roll, hidden like a secret that didn't want to be kept but couldn't risk being known. She didn't need to see it to picture it. trexium-core, Vanguard stock, the barrel long and matte, the casing smoothed down where fingers had once gripped it over and over again. She had only seen the glow twice, but it stayed with her—a soft pulse, unnatural and quiet, like something alive that refused to speak.

Her father had said it wasn't his. He hadn't looked at her when he said it.

She sat back, resting her spine against the cold frame, her legs pulled in close. Outside the walls, wind swept through the compound's perimeter shields, pulling low whines from the tension wires. Inside, everything hummed—quiet, steady, and temporary.

She listened for the sounds that always came, eventually. The soft click of boots in the hall. The tap of metal on concrete. The way a weapon shifted on someone's back when they turned a corner and didn't expect to be seen.

She didn't sleep. Not because of fear. Not because of noise.

Because something in her knew—deep in the marrow—that even behind these walls, nothing lasted.

The snowmelt behind the mess unit had become a game board again. Daryas wobbled along the length of the elevated pipe, arms out, trying to keep her balance as Parker and Chella shouted encouragement from a crate stack near the edge of the maintenance yard.

"You're over the line!" Chella called, grinning as she clutched her ration bar like it was a trophy. "You drop now, and I get the rest of your biscuit."

"Not a chance," Daryas shot back, stepping carefully over a patch of frost crusting the pipe's seam. "I already paid half for slipping yesterday."

"This is your redemption arc," Parker said, arms folded, the kind of dramatic tone he used whenever he quoted lines from old training footage. "Fall with style, and it still counts."

She didn't fall.

Not right away, anyway.

She made it three steps farther, lips pulled into a tight smile, before the echo of something low and mechanical drifted down the corridor behind them. It was subtle at first, more a hum than a sound—like a generator engaging or a drone warming up.

They all paused.

The stronghold's intercom popped, then crackled—static, then a word she couldn't make out. Then the alarm hit.

A triple pulse. Not a drill.

The smiles vanished. Chella dropped her bar. Parker swore under his breath. Daryas jumped down, landing awkwardly and rolling through the melt.

People were shouting now. Doors opened. Metal slammed. Orders came fast, but not fast enough to make sense of them. Through the corridor to the eastern scaffolds, Daryas glimpsed a flicker of movement in the sky. Then another.

And then screaming.

A figure crashed onto the upper deck above the utility platform, limbs flailing as it skidded off the edge and disappeared from view. Another figure dove after it—this one wasn't human. Not anymore.

Wings. Black and wide, torn in places like old canvas. The flyer jerked through the air, a scream tearing through the air like it had no lungs left but hadn't yet noticed.

Then another scream, from lower—closer. One of the younger sentries ran past them, breath ragged, yelling something about the east wall. Something about them being inside.

Daryas didn't wait. Her instincts pulled her forward. The others turned toward the bunker—toward safety. She ran the opposite way.

The firing range gates were half-open. She ducked through them, boots slipping in the frost. The shrieks overhead had multiplied. More than one flyer now—at least five, maybe more. Their shadows darted across the compound like birds too large to belong to the world anymore.

The sky above the walls was chaos. Flashing bursts of trexium fire lit the clouds pink and blue. Two flyers collided mid-air, one spinning off into the woods, the other diving with purpose. Ground walkers surged at the gates below, clawing at the fencing, their bodies smashing into the barricades with no care for the ones in front.

Daryas scrambled across the range. The storage unit on the left had been left unsecured—someone panicked, forgot protocol. Rifles inside, at least a dozen, stacked but not locked. Her hands moved without thinking.

One rifle. Loaded. No time to check the magazine for rounds the way her mother had taught her.

A shriek above her head. Dust rained down from the support trusses.

She rolled behind a sandbag and peeked up just in time to see the flyer swoop, wingspan blotting out what little light was left. Its body was twisted, the remnants of a uniform still clinging to one shoulder. Its face was ruined, torn open around a permanent snarl, its eyes glowing like a flare just before it burns out.

She fired.

The stock of the rifle hammered into her shoulder. She winced with pain but pushed through it. She had felt worse.

The round clipped its wing. Not enough. It veered hard, recovered, then dove again.

She ran.

Her feet pounded across the concrete, her lungs tight from cold and fear. Another scream—this one human, somewhere behind her. Then the bark of gunfire. Then another impact, something heavy slamming into the roof of the range. She turned and fired again, feeling the gun hammering into her already sore shoulder.

This time, the shot hit square.

The flyer jerked mid-dive, spiraled. Its claws tore a gash in the tarp above her before its body hit the ground with a sickening crunch, wings folding like broken scaffolding beneath it.

She stood over it for a moment, breathing hard, chest heaving.

It wasn't moving.

She could still hear the others—flyers, shrieks, screams of the dying—but this one was gone. The glow in its eyes had faded.

And something in her, deep in her chest, relaxed.

She should've dropped the gun and run. Instead, she stared for just a few seconds longer. At the stillness. At the thing that had taken so much from so many.

Then she laid the rifle gently beside the body and turned toward the inner gates, where the reinforced bunker doors had just begun to seal.

She ran.

The gates were closing—slower than they should have. A child tripped in front of her. Daryas grabbed her arm and hauled her up, dragging them both through the entry just before the steel slammed into place behind them.

Inside the bunker, it was warm and quiet.

She didn't speak. She didn't cry. She found a place against the wall and sat with her knees pulled to her chest, the press of the girl's hand still lingering on her arm.

All around her, families whispered. Others sobbed. Some just stared. Daryas watched the door. Her hands trembled and her shoulder ached, but she just thought of the flyer. The way its eyes stopped glowing.

How, for in that moment, she had felt like something being made right.

Chapter 3 – Before the Break

The rifle kicked back against Daryas' shoulder harder than she expected, but she didn't flinch. She adjusted her grip, reset her stance, and fired again—upper chest target, clean shot. The dummy lurched on its post, torn fabric fluttering from the impact. She lowered the weapon, rolled her shoulders once, and stepped back to let the next cadet through.

The range was hot this cycle, the heat radiating off the sandbags and synthetic matting, making the air shimmer just above the ground. Sweat pooled between her shoulder blades, soaked through the back of her collar, but she didn't notice it anymore. Not really. Her body had learned to ignore discomfort in favor of precision.

"Again."

The instructor's voice was clipped but satisfied. He didn't say much more than that anymore. With Daryas, he didn't need to.

She moved back to the line.

Beside her, Brit adjusted the strap on her rig and slapped the side of her rifle like it had insulted her. Her blonde hair was braided back tight, but the streak of purple was always there—cut straight through the braid like a signal flare. A matching line of violet face paint swept from cheek to temple, bold and unmistakable.

"You gonna hit center mass this time, or you just here to look intimidating?" Brit grinned.

Daryas gave her a sideways glance. "One of us has to look good."

"True. But only one of us makes it look easy."

They loaded together in sync, stepping back to the line. The wind picked up just a little—enough to stir the flags on the outposts, enough to carry the scent of ozone and old oil from the various towers and repair bays. Training ranges always smelled the same, no matter the move: sweat, smoke, dust, and the faint sting of scorched polymers.

The instructor raised a hand. "Three-round drill. Moving targets. Clear your sectors."

The dummies began to move—shuffled tracks through the sand, their forms jerking unpredictably. Daryas leveled her rifle and fired with practiced speed. One. Two. Three. The head on her third target snapped back, and the dummy spun once before collapsing.

Beside her, Brit shouted, "Got 'em!" and blew an exaggerated kiss at her last target. "Purple wins again."

They filed off the line and dropped into a crouch near the munitions bin. Brit tore open a ration bar and split it down the seam before tossing half into Daryas' lap.

"You were breathing off pace on your first shot," Brit said, unwrapping her own half. "You correct?"

"Grip was tight. Should've eased on the trigger pull."

"Mm." Brit chewed thoughtfully. "We're gonna need to start leading movement drills. Some of the new ones are slow—like 'lose-you-at-the-gate' slow."

Daryas nodded. She'd noticed too.

"Think this base will hold?" Brit asked, voice quieter now, though still casual. "Feels like we've been here too long. Last move was four weeks ago. Five, if you count the delay in resupply."

"Commander hasn't pushed the call yet."

"Let's hope that's a good thing."

They sat in silence for a moment, heads tilted back against the rough wall behind them. Overhead, a pair of scout flyers buzzed across the sky—real ones, this time. Manned. Human. The sound of their engines always made Daryas pause.

She hadn't seen an undead flyer since she was twelve. But she remembered every detail.

"Think about it much?" Brit asked, wiping a smudge from her purple-painted cheek. "What it'd be like? Getting picked?"

"For Vanguard?"

"Yeah." Brit pulled her braid tighter, securing the tie. "They're ghosts out there. Armor's built for more than protection. It's meant to be legend. One of them visited the gate last week. I didn't see his face, but the armor was violet—deep. Like night."

Daryas said nothing.

Brit leaned her head back, closed her eyes. "They say if you make it in, you don't just get the armor. You get the choice. Where to go. What to take on. What missions to lead."

"They don't make the choices," Daryas said. "They just get sent first. Or last."

"Maybe." Brit opened one eye. "But they still get remembered."

They fell quiet again, each lost in her own thoughts. The heat had eased a little, shadows growing longer across the range as the day tilted toward evening. Daryas watched Brit lean into the moment—face tilted to the light, that streak of purple catching the sun just right.

Daryas didn't smile much anymore. Not really. But she allowed herself one now.

"I'm not slowing down for you," she said.

Brit grinned. "Wouldn't ask you to."

The range was quiet by the time Daryas finished cleaning down her rifle. The others had already filed out, some to bunk, others to drills, but she stayed behind, wiping down the bolt casing with a cloth that smelled like grease and heat and the inside of her father's jacket. Brit had taken off ahead of her, joking about beating the food line before the rehydrated stew turned into glue, but Daryas moved slower, more methodically, like she wasn't ready to let go of the weight in her hands just yet.

Outside, the air was cooler. The sun hovered just above the compound wall, stretching long shadows down the corridor between the training yard and the quartermaster station. She cut across the walkway behind the vehicle bay and stepped into the hum of base life—boots thudding against catwalks, the low bark of orders from upper decks, someone cursing in the distance over a jammed lift. It wasn't chaotic. Not yet. But it never felt settled, either. Just in motion.

She passed two engineers pulling cable from a broken perimeter drone and slipped through a side entrance into the armory where her father worked maintenance. The sharp smell of metal and ion discharge hit her first, followed by the subtle hint of antiseptic from the medtech station across the hall. The lights inside were dimmed low to preserve power. Tools hung in neat rows above each bench. Weapon casings, partially disassembled, lay in the cradles, guts exposed and ready for reassembly.

Her father stood at the far end, hunched slightly over a trexium power cell, hands wrapped in fingerless gloves as he filed the casing along its seam. His eyes flicked up the moment she entered.

"Still warm out?" he asked without looking back down.

"Cooling off. You missed it—we drilled moving targets today. Brit smoked one of the instructors on reflex."

He grunted, not unkindly. "She's sharp. You're faster."

Daryas pulled herself up onto the workbench beside him, resting her boots against a bin of spare grips. For a moment, they sat in silence, the rhythmic hiss of the file dragging across the metal filling the space between them. She watched the way he moved, careful and exact, hands steady even with the old scar near his knuckle that never fully healed from the breach back in Move Nine.

He set the tool aside and rotated the core until the light caught the casing just right. It pulsed faintly—just a sliver of pink shimmer beneath the surface. The kind of glow that meant it still worked, but not forever.

"You keeping it balanced?" she asked.

"As much as it'll let me." He paused, thumb brushing the edge. "This one's temperamental. Like the person who keeps checking the drawer I store it in."

She didn't look away. "Just checking it's still there."

His expression didn't change. But he didn't scold her either.

"Not everyone trusts the walls," he said.

"They shouldn't," she replied.

He nodded once and slid the core back into its housing, the glow disappearing as he locked the chamber shut. "You and Brit still talking about becoming Vanguard?"

"Sometimes."

"She thinks she can make it?"

"She wants it."

He wiped his hands clean and leaned back, resting against the bench like the weight of the day had finally caught up to him. "Just make sure it's not the only thing 'she' wants."

Daryas didn't answer. Her father could always tell when she wasn't being entirely up front.

After a moment, she pushed off the bench and made her way toward the exit. As she reached the doorway, she paused and looked back.

"You think I'd make it?"

"To Vanguard?"

She nodded once.

Her father studied her—not like a soldier. Like a father who didn't know whether his answer would help or hurt. The scar on his face catching the light, feeling like a ravine of memory stretched along its length.

"You're not done becoming who you are yet," he said. "But if you keep heading that direction… yeah. You'll make it."

She held his gaze a moment longer, then left without another word.

The mess was half full by the time she reached it. Rows of benches lined the central atrium, overhead lights buzzing faintly in the places where the wiring had gone bad. Steam rose from the food line. She spotted Brit near the back, feet up on the bench, pulling her braid tighter while a young tech scrubbed grime off her armor plates.

"There she is," Brit said as Daryas dropped onto the bench across from her. "Thought you fell into the recycler."

"Armory. My dad had the core open."

"Did you ask?"

Daryas didn't answer. Brit grinned like that was answer enough.

They ate quietly, swapping training stories and speculating about the next move—how soon it might come, how far they'd go. Brit talked about her sister, who'd been stationed two strongholds back and had once run logistics on a Vanguard supply route. She described it like myth, like her sister had glimpsed the other side of the curtain where decisions were made and legends were built.

"And the gear," Brit said, licking broth from her thumb. "It's not just for show. Did you know they run heat-dispersal threading through the armor plates? You don't even feel the charge when you fire. It just bleeds out."

"Wouldn't matter," Daryas said, tossing her empty tray into the bin beside them. "As long as it drops the target."

Brit smiled. "You'd look good in purple."

Daryas raised an eyebrow. "You mean the hair?"

"I mean the paint. The armor. The Vanguard colors."

"I'm not picking colors until I know I'm gonna make it. Getting hopes up doesn't do anyone any good."

"That's okay." Brit swiped a streak of purple across her own cheek with the last bit of face paint from her pouch. "I'll pick for both of us."

Chapter 4 – The Cost of Friendship

The gate opened slowly, one half dragging slightly against its track, the other steady as it pulled wide. A gust of dry summer air swept through the corridor, thick with dust and the scent of sun-baked dirt, warm stone, and long-stewed compost. It carried the steady lowing of cattle and the rustle of penned sheep just outside the walls. The livestock fields wrapped along the southern perimeter—pigs in low pens, chickens scratching at bare patches of dirt, cattle clustered near the troughs. Rows of fencing ringed the farm plots, reinforced not just against walkers but the occasional raider hoping to steal meat or seed grain.

Farmhands moved between the enclosures, work-roughened hands and heavy boots, sun-creased faces turned toward their work without looking up. It wasn't showy labor, but it kept the stronghold alive. Daryas had helped once, back during her early assignments—just long enough to know she didn't want to shovel troughs for a living. Still, she respected it. Every part mattered.

Today, her place wasn't among the pens. It was on the rig.

She stood near the rear, helmet tucked under one arm, fingers curled lightly around the base as the last few trainees climbed aboard. Sweat already clung to her skin beneath her collar, gathering along her spine beneath the padded armor lining. Her hair, braided back, still frizzed from the heat, strands curling loose against her neck.

Twelve trainees. This was their first live deployment.

No more simulations. No more dummies. The undead were out there. This would be their first taste of real blood.

Brit stood beside her, one boot on the loading ramp, twisting the purple-streaked braid between her fingers. The morning sun caught the color just right, gleaming against her tanned skin. A fresh smear of violet paint angled across her cheekbone like a brand.

"You think they'll put us in front?" she asked, half-grin already forming.

"We're not that lucky," Daryas replied.

"Speak for yourself."

The transport gave a low groan as the engine surged, and the rig began to roll. Beneath their boots, the floor shuddered once, then steadied. They moved past the outer livestock pens and through the gates. Beyond the fencing, the land stretched wide and sun-hardened, spotted with brush and brittle trees, their shadows sharp and short beneath the midday sun.

Inside the rig, heat clung like a second layer of armor. Fans pushed warm air around without cooling anything. The twelve of them sat opposite each other in rows—helmets off, rifles between knees, armor lined with dust and polish. Some stared at nothing. Others adjusted gear with nervous hands. A few cracked quiet jokes, but the laughter didn't last long.

Five Vanguards stood at intervals—two at the front, two at the rear, one stationed dead center. Their armor set them apart immediately—reinforced plates, blackened visors, movement as precise and weightless as memory. They spoke little, checking straps, adjusting weapons, nodding at each other in subtle rhythms. They didn't radiate intimidation. They didn't need to.

One of them, positioned center-left, rested a hand lightly on the overhead rail as the rig shifted over uneven trail. He hadn't spoken since boarding, but he hadn't needed to. The way the others oriented around him—not out of command, but as habit—told Daryas enough. When the ride hit a rough patch, people glanced at him first. He didn't flinch. Didn't shift.

Anchor.

Brit nudged her gently. "That one's the kind they write songs about."

"Sure," Daryas murmured, adjusting her rifle strap. "You'll be the one who sings it?"

"I'll paint it," Brit said, tapping her face paint with two fingers. "Faster."

The rig rumbled on.

The path wound between patches of coarse grass and scrub pine, the kind of growth that shot up fast in early summer and stayed brittle and yellow by midseason. The air smelled of dust and distant pollen, layered with the chemical tang of old trexium residue baked into the rig's walls.

Through the narrow vent slits, Daryas caught glimpses of the terrain. Movement to the right—something large darting through the brush. Four legs, long frame, lean shoulders.

"Deer," Brit muttered. "Maybe elk."

"Farther than they usually range."

"Guess they're running out of shade too."

Sometimes hunting teams brought back a fresh kill—deer, rabbits, once even a wild hog. It didn't replace the pens, but it gave the cooks something better to work with. Something that made a meal feel earned. It was dangerous work though, inevitably drawing unwanted attention from the larger threat beyond the walls.

The rig slowed near a fork in the path. A reconfiguration marker stood near the split, just a short metal pole marked with faded blue paint. Last stronghold zone. Beyond that, open patrol territory.

The Vanguards moved first.

One dropped silently from the rear ramp, sweeping the treeline with a shoulder-mounted scanner. Another gave the signal. The rig came to a full stop.

The voice came from the front—firm, low, unhurried.

"Out. Final checks. Gear ready. Pairs stay close. No contact until the call."

Boots hit dirt. Daryas followed Brit down the ramp and into the dry heat. The wind carried grit across the flat of her tongue. Brit slid her helmet into place, locked the strap, and gave a low whistle.

"Smells like work."

Ahead, the Vanguard in the center turned toward the trainees and spoke again. "Confirmed group yesterday. Twelve undead. Slow. Spread formation. You move in two pairs per wedge. Call out anything that shifts. Your assignment—forward recon."

He pointed to Daryas and Brit.

Daryas adjusted her grip. Brit smirked, eyes already forward.

"Let's go," Brit said.

The trees began to close in as they moved deeper into the quadrant. Sunlight filtered through the canopy in patches, dappling the undergrowth in gold and shadow, but the heat lingered, heavy and close. Brit's boots kicked through dry brush as she advanced on point, three paces ahead of Daryas, moving with the steady confidence of someone who had drilled this route in her sleep. Daryas kept close, watching the angles, the rhythm of movement, the spaces between them that allowed freedom and protection both.

Sweat soaked the back of her collar where the armor pressed tight against her neck, but she barely registered the discomfort. Her rifle sat snug against her shoulder, the strap running across her chest as she kept the muzzle low and her eyes high. They'd been briefed on the projected contact zone—small group, slow walkers, low risk—but protocol didn't care what was expected. It only cared what was missed.

A few meters ahead, Brit paused and crouched beside a broken patch of underbrush. She held up two fingers and pointed to the dirt. Daryas followed the signal and moved beside her, keeping one eye on the trees as she dropped to a knee.

A faint trail carved through the undergrowth—shallow depressions in the soil, uneven spacing, wide footfalls. Bare tracks. No tread marks.

"Walker," Brit murmured.

Daryas nodded and studied the bend in the path where the trail angled west. The spacing suggested a dragging gait, but not staggered. Steady movement. Intentional or not, it meant the thing had been walking for a while without slowing.

She tapped her comm and spoke low. "Movement sign confirmed. Single track. Barefoot. Heading west-northwest. No sign of decay."

The comm crackled with the return. "Confirmed. Forward pair stays on trail. Squad breaking wedge, staggered support. Be advised—trail may fork. Maintain visual."

Brit stood first, brushing her fingers along the edge of her braid as she scanned the trees ahead. "Lead position. Finally. Let's see what it feels like to be important."

Daryas didn't smile, but she took point without hesitation, shifting her grip as they began to advance again through the thinning woods. The trees here were taller, with bare trunks reaching up like twisted poles, their upper branches tangled into a half-canopy that filtered light into long, slanted beams. The buzz of insects pressed in from the sides, thicker than before, and the birds that had accompanied their entry had long since gone quiet.

Somewhere to her right, something large moved through the brush—too quiet for panic, too smooth for wind. Her hand tensed over the grip of her rifle, but when the movement passed without return, she kept going. She knew the feeling settling into her chest. It wasn't fear. It was the instinct that came before it— awareness sharpening, perception narrowing.

Up ahead, the brush shifted again.

She dropped into a crouch, raising a fist to halt. Brit stopped behind her, eyes already scanning.

They saw the shapes at the same time.

They moved slowly between the trees, half-hidden by undergrowth and shadow. Not charging. Not sprinting. Just walking—steady, straight, and unflinching. Seven. No, eight. Possibly more behind the trees. Pale skin, bloodless. Their expressions were blank, mouths slightly open but soundless. No decay, no damage. Just vacancy. Like something human had been turned off, and the result had never noticed.

The lead walker passed through a shaft of sunlight, and Daryas caught the smooth, unbroken skin along its cheek. The eyes were wide and unfocused, not glassy but distant, like staring at something far behind the present.

They didn't hesitate. Daryas raised her rifle and fired a single shot. The round struck clean—center mass on the skull—and the walker dropped, legs folding beneath it.

Brit stepped forward and fired twice. The first shot staggered a second target, the second hit its mark. Dull thuds followed as bodies hit the dirt and rolled down a small slope behind the trail.

The others didn't panic. They didn't cry out. They simply shifted toward the new direction of noise. Their limbs moved with loose fluidity, nothing jerky or wild, but not cautious either. It was like watching something that didn't understand injury, didn't remember fear.

The squad moved quickly to back them up, boots pressing through soft ground as cover fire rang out. The shots came crisp and clean, each burst coordinated by the Vanguard on comm, whose voice remained even, measured, deliberate.

Daryas moved to flank left, covering Brit's advance as she dropped another target with a burst to the chest, followed by a headshot. One of the walkers veered too close, and Daryas swung her rifle up, firing once into the base of its neck. The body collapsed instantly.

Then, silence.

The final shot echoed longer than expected, the crack of it rolling through the brush until it was swallowed by the stillness that followed. Brit exhaled sharply and turned in a slow circle, checking every direction twice.

"All down," she said. "That's all of them."

Daryas stayed crouched, breathing through her nose, eyes narrowing on the trail ahead. Something didn't sit right.

"They weren't scattered," she said. "They were waiting."

"Waiting?" Brit asked.

Daryas pointed to the line they'd followed. "The trail led us straight to them. It wasn't a chance run-in. It was a funnel."

Brit lowered her rifle slightly and followed the line of sight. The grass was disturbed in one long sweep, footpaths crossing at strange angles that didn't make sense for a natural shuffle. Too deliberate. Too clean.

The comms clicked again. "Delta team, sweep the left and confirm no stragglers. Hold your position until Alpha regroups."

Daryas acknowledged the call and stood slowly, eyes still on the treeline beyond the clearing.

"We're not done here," she said quietly.

And somewhere ahead, behind the line of trees and the rustling leaves that no longer sounded like wind, something else had started moving.

The call came over comms low and clipped, just sharp enough to cut through the weight in the air.

"Secondary group incoming—northwest brushline. Tight formation. More than initial count. Regroup east ridge."

Daryas didn't need the numbers to know something was wrong. From where she crouched above the shallow basin, she could already see movement threading through the treeline—not the slow, scattered shuffling they'd drilled for, but a broad sweep of pale bodies moving in eerie coordination. They weren't running, weren't even accelerating, but they came with an undeniable purpose. Shoulders loose, arms swaying in the heat, heads fixed forward with vacant focus, like whatever animated them had only one direction and didn't care how much noise it made getting there.

One of the Vanguard repositioned across the line, his armor casting faint reflections as he moved—soft pink highlights pulsing along the seams of his plating where the trexium core burned steadily beneath. His weapon glowed just as faintly through the vents in its barrel, and when he raised it, the pink shimmer at the trigger chamber swelled brighter, casting flashes across his gauntlet as he fired. The first few walkers dropped instantly, limbs folding as they hit the dirt, clean and quiet. Another Vanguard flanked the rise, keeping their arc covered, their presence solid and silent—five of them in all, shifting like clockwork among the crumbling formation.

But the wave didn't break.

The undead kept coming, more than they'd counted, more than they'd accounted for. And this time, they weren't spaced or distracted. They advanced together, coordinated without noise or urgency, their dead faces blank and their eyes wide open, as if something inside was watching even if it couldn't speak.

The trainees held as long as they could. Shots rang out in short bursts, the air filling with the scent of scorched powder and hot grass. Brit moved in perfect rhythm beside Daryas, rifle steady, breath even, her painted cheek flushed with heat as she turned and dropped another target at ten paces. Daryas mirrored the movement, pivoting left to cover the flank, her shots landing solidly in the skulls of the two that came closest. One of them collapsed just inches from her boot, its eyes staring up at her in the exact same way they had before the bullet hit—empty, absent, unblinking.

Then came the break.

A trainee on their left screamed as the line collapsed. Daryas saw him fall, hands up, rifle half-raised, and then the undead were on him. Another staggered back, bleeding from a bite that had torn through the seam in his armor. The formation crumbled in seconds, and what had been a disciplined maneuver dissolved into scattered motion and shouting voices.

She and Brit fell back together, shoulder to shoulder, firing in short, measured bursts. The Vanguard team called for a regroup at the eastern ridge, but it was already too late to reform. The dead were pressing in from all sides, and the path they'd come from was no longer open.

Daryas caught a glimpse of one of the Vanguards issuing a command she couldn't hear over the comm interference, then signaling toward the sky—an extract call. The rig must have already started its return cycle. The only way out now was to hold until the Vanguards could clear a path or reinforcements arrived.

They pivoted again—Daryas firing, Brit reloading—and then the gap between them opened.

Daryas turned just in time to see Brit go down, her rifle spinning across the dirt as two walkers hit her from opposite sides. The impact forced her to the ground, armor scraping hard across the cracked basin floor as she kicked out to break the grip of the first. One of the undead fell backward under the force, but the other remained, landing heavily atop her, its weight driving her down and pinning her arm.

Daryas reacted before she thought, sprinting forward, firing twice to clear her approach, and slamming into the creature with enough force to knock it off Brit's chest. She dragged her friend halfway to her knees, but Brit was already bleeding badly—red blooming along her midsection where armor had split from the fall or from the clawed hands that had tried to tear her open.

They staggered backward together, but Daryas couldn't hold her. Brit's weight shifted, and she slumped sideways, her mouth open as she tried to speak.

Daryas dropped beside her, hands slick with blood now, trying to press the torn armor back into place as if that would hold the life inside. Brit looked at her—not with fear, but with confusion. Her hand lifted just barely before falling again.

The wave wasn't stopping.

Daryas turned, firing her last rounds in blind succession. When the rifle clicked dry, she didn't hesitate. Her hand dropped to her thigh sheath, fingers wrapping around the hilt of the long blade she carried, a comfort since the day they let her keep it.

She rose without thinking, blade drawn, and charged into the crush of bodies.

There was no more formation. No more comms. No orders. No teammates. Just the rhythm of movement—parry, stab, pivot, strike—and the sound of breathing that wasn't hers. She moved with no memory of how long. Her arm ached, her shoulders burned, but she didn't stop. When one fell, another filled the space, and she met them with blade and bone and the fire behind her ribs that had started the moment Brit had been pulled away.

Eventually, the last one fell.

And the silence that followed felt wrong.

She stood in the clearing, surrounded by bodies—uniformed, unrecognizable, too many to count—and she knew only one name among them.

She turned, scanning the wreckage, breath coming hard now, her muscles trembling from effort and adrenaline. Her blade hung low in her grip, streaked with blood and dirt, her other hand clutching the air like it still expected another shape to come for her.

Then something shifted behind her.

The sound was soft. A breath, maybe. A shuffle.

She turned slowly, her gaze finding the figure where she had left her.

Brit was rising.

One arm twisted at the elbow, one leg dragging behind her, her body jerking with small, disjointed motions as if her nerves had forgotten how to move. Her face was pale now, nearly colorless, and the purple streak in her braid had smeared across her cheek like paint left out in the rain.

Daryas stepped back, lips parting with a cry that broke halfway up her throat, but no sound followed.

No help answered. No shots rang out. The rest had moved, had fought, had retreated. She was alone.

Brit took a step forward—slow, aimless, her eyes half-lidded and vacant.

There was no recognition, no life. Just an awful, yawning stillness behind her face.

Daryas raised her knife. Not out of anger. Not even out of fear. The thought brought tears to her eyes, but she knew in that moment there was nothing left to do.

Chapter 5 – A Name to Remember

The basin was quiet now, filled only with the low hum of distant flyers and the quiet settling of bodies cooling in the heat. Daryas sat with her back against a stone outcrop near the wall's broken edge, legs bent, arms slack in her lap. Her knife was still buried in Brit's chest, the hilt tilted slightly where her grip had finally relaxed. She hadn't moved since.

Brit's head rested on her shoulder at an unnatural angle. The braid—still streaked faintly with violet—frayed at the end, the color dulled where blood had soaked through. Her eyes no longer opened. Her face had gone slack, peaceful in a way that felt cruel.

Daryas didn't remember how long she had been there. The sun had shifted; the shadows lengthening as heat pooled in the hollowed dirt around them. The smell of blood lingered like iron and earth and ash, and the taste of it clung to the back of her throat. Somewhere nearby, flies buzzed over scorched armor, but they didn't come close to her.

She heard boots approaching. Controlled, deliberate. The kind of step that meant someone wasn't in a hurry but always arrived exactly when they meant to.

She didn't look up.

A quiet voice came through the distortion of a Vanguard's external comms.

"Found her. South wall. She's alive."

A pause followed. Faint comms chatter answered, too low to hear.

Then the voice came again, lower this time, spoken directly. "You hurt?"

Daryas didn't answer. She didn't even flinch.

The man didn't press her. The armor shifted once as he knelt beside her, visor tilted slightly in her direction, his presence calm, steady. He didn't speak again until he reached out—not forcefully, not demanding. Just a gloved hand, held open on his knee, palm up, waiting.

She stared at it for a while, then placed her hand in his.

He didn't pull.

He helped her rise slowly, keeping pace with her balance as her knees threatened to give. She stumbled once as her boot caught in the dirt, but his grip held firm, steadying her until she stood fully upright. Her knife stayed where it was. Neither of them looked at it.

They walked in silence. The clearing stretched around them, scattered with too many fallen forms to count. Some were trainees, others walkers, but none were moving anymore. The wind had picked up slightly, dragging grit across the surface of her boots, kicking up the scent of scorched gear and heat-struck grass.

The small air transport had landed just beyond the ridge—a low-slung military flier, built more for speed than cargo. The hatch remained open as a second Vanguard waited beside it, his weapon low and posture loose. No one rushed her. No one tried to talk.

The man at her side—armor trimmed in red, marked cleanly with stylized cuts across the shoulders and chest—walked with her in silence. She climbed aboard slowly, her limbs stiff and her shoulders heavy, every movement dulled by the ache of exhaustion that had settled deep in her bones. He followed, taking the bench across from her, his helmet resting on the floor by his boots.

The light from the cabin strips caught the red trim of his armor as he sat forward slightly, elbows on his knees, his posture composed but not closed. It wasn't arrogance—just presence.

For a long moment, they didn't speak.

Then, without a word, he reached up and removed his helmet. The hiss of the pressure seal broke softly, releasing a faint curl of air as the locking clasps gave way. He set the helmet down between his boots and brushed a hand back through hair damp with sweat; the strands shifting slightly before settling in place. His face was lined—not with age, but with time. It was a face carved by years of duty, shaped by field wind and battle silence. And yet, something about him remained open. Steady. Not hardened. Not yet.

"You held your ground," he said.

There was no disbelief in the words. No awe. Just quiet recognition, offered without ceremony.

Daryas didn't respond. Her eyes stayed on the floor between them, locked on some point that didn't exist.

"I counted at least fifteen around you," he continued, voice calm. "Most of them close. That's not a team effort. That was you."

She shifted her gaze to the side viewport, watching the ridgeline begin to fade as the flier lifted. The horizon spread out ahead of them, smoke still curling in thin lines from where the last bodies had fallen.

Her hands rested in her lap, fingers caked in dried blood, her knuckles scraped raw. She wasn't shaking anymore, but she couldn't unclench her grip.

"Three of you made it out alive," he said after a moment.

Still, she said nothing. Her mouth was dry. Her throat felt raw, like she'd been screaming, though she couldn't remember if she had. The silence hung between them—not empty, but heavy, like a conversation that had already happened in another life.

Eventually, her voice came, quieter than she meant.

"She wanted Vanguard armor in purple."

He looked at her—not surprised, not searching for meaning—but with something like understanding settling behind his eyes.

"She would've worn it well," he said.

"She earned it," Daryas replied.

Her voice didn't break.

The flier banked to the left, and the light from the high windows broke across the cabin in long golden slashes. Dust floated through the beams, catching the shift and shimmer of motion before it all settled again.

They rode like that for a while—quiet, steady, without the need to fill space with anything more. Then a soft comm vibration came from his wrist. He checked it, his expression shifting subtly.

"Base commander," he said, mostly to himself. He stood slowly and turned toward the hatch at the rear of the cabin. Before leaving, he looked back at her.

"I'll be back in a few. I'll have someone come sit with you, so you're not alone."

He stepped through the rear, the door hissing closed behind him. The red trim of his armor caught a last flicker of sunlight before the seal locked.

Another Vanguard stepped in a moment later—his armor older, worn to a dull matte, one shoulder strap frayed from overuse. He didn't ask questions. He just crossed the cabin and eased down onto the bench beside her.

"Achilles," he said, as if they'd already met. His voice was even, relaxed, not formal but not careless either. "He asked me to sit with you. Figured it's better to be quiet with someone than by yourself."

Daryas nodded faintly.

They sat that way for a while. No one filled the space too quickly. The wind outside stirred now and then, brushing against the hull with a faint, rhythmic pulse.

Achilles broke the silence gently.

"I heard you were found next to your friend. You want to tell me about her?"

Daryas let out a breath she hadn't realized she'd been holding.

"She was fast," she said. "She used to win every foot drill, even against people bigger than her."

"She the one with the purple paint?" he asked.

Daryas nodded again.

"She wanted Vanguard armor in purple," she said softly. "Not for attention. She just wanted to make something her own."

Achilles leaned forward, hands clasped loosely. "That sounds like someone who was going to make a mark."

"She did."

Her voice cracked slightly then. Just a thread of it. She pressed her thumb against her palm to keep it from spreading.

"She went down hard," she added. "I tried to drag her back. I really tried."

"You did," Achilles said, without hesitation. "I saw the report."

Daryas stared at her hands again, her shoulders slowly curling forward under a weight that wouldn't lift.

"She was better than me," she said.

"No," Achilles replied. "She was different."

She didn't answer, but her eyes closed for a second longer than a blink.

"He found me," she said quietly. "After all that."

Achilles nodded. "Yeah. Standard post-battle patrol. You weren't the only one left behind. But... you were the only one who made it on foot."

"Who is he?"

Achilles smiled faintly, then glanced over his shoulder toward the back of the flier.

"He's not the type who likes people talking about him. But I guess it doesn't count if he's not in the room."

Daryas didn't move.

"He came up as a farmer," Achilles began. "Grain, livestock, irrigation. Just another labor post outside a no-name stronghold. One of the first hit during the fall there. I wasn't there, but I heard that when the walls broke, he didn't run. Didn't freeze. He fought."

She listened. She didn't interrupt.

"He pulled six people out by hand. No gear. No weapon. Burned his hands open dragging a child out of the admin center. When help arrived, he was still holding what was left of the perimeter with a broken shovel and a steel door hinge. Took out four walkers that way."

Achilles shook his head, not in disbelief, but in reverence.

"He didn't want rank. Didn't even apply for training. But our base commander saw what he was made of. Pulled strings. He passed every trial without complaint. And now? Best Vanguard squad in the whole damn valley. He personally leads every mission his team launches from the front."

"You on his team?" Daryas asked quietly.

Achilles laughed.

"Ha, I wish. Nah, I'm on a recon team. Was asked to come along to help find the survivors and get them out."

Daryas turned slowly toward the rear of the cabin.

The door had opened again. By the open bay hatch, the red-hued vanguard stood alone, the wind cutting through his hair as he stared out over the fields, light catching the lines of his armor. The land drifted beneath them in long, sweeping curves of forest and field, dark rivers weaving silver between the ridgelines. He stood like a statue—silent, watchful, whole.

Daryas spoke without turning back.

"What's his name?"

Achilles looked over to see the man standing silhouetted against the moving landscape below. His reply was almost reverent.

"Varek."

Chapter 6 – Steel and Violet

A long-forgotten impact cracked the mirror in the upper corner, creating a spiderweb of fine fractures. Daryas stared into it anyway, drawing the thin streak of purple through her braid with careful precision. The dye was old, stretched thin between years of use, but the color still burned against her dark hair—sharp and deliberate.

Five years. Five years since the day she buried her knife in the chest of someone who had once been as good as family. Five years of waking up, weaving that line of color through her hair, and carrying it into every drill, every patrol, every deployment that followed. It wasn't superstition. It wasn't even tradition. It was a tether. A promise she hadn't dared break.

She cinched the braid tight, securing the end with a thin strip of reinforced thread, and leaned back from the mirror. The armor fit better now—Vanguard trainee plating, not the loaned gear of a child surviving on borrowed time. She moved differently, too. The mirror didn't show it, not exactly, but she could feel it in her hands and in the way the armor sat across her shoulders. She wasn't waiting to become something anymore. She was standing in it.

The barracks around her hummed with morning life. Voices drifted through the thin corridor walls, low and steady—soldiers swapping last-minute gear, checking weapons, trading half-hearted bets on the day's training rotations. Outside, she could hear the clatter of boots on the main catwalks and the occasional bark of instruction rising from the open training yard.

The Coalition strongholds had changed too, though not in ways the maps bothered to mark. Fewer formal lines. More rapid shifts between sectors. Faster rotations, leaner supply lines. Always moving, always clearing, always surviving. It wasn't a place for permanence, but it was one that remembered names when it needed to.

And some names carried heavier now than others.

Commander Varek's name carried like that—spoken low in planning rooms, half-muttered with respect or calculation or both. He wasn't officially Base Commander yet, not on paper. But anyone with eyes knew it was only a matter of time. The old commander had died three moves ago—an infection caught during a patrol sweep that no one had seen coming—and when the chain of command had shifted, there'd been no arguments. Varek stepped up the way he stepped into everything: quietly, completely.

He had been the first person to reach her after Brit's death. The first hand to pull her up off the ground when she hadn't trusted herself to stand. She hadn't forgotten.

She pulled the last strap tight on her chest rig, flexed her shoulders once, and stepped into the corridor.

The morning smelled of sweat and damp stone, of hot wiring and recycled air and the faint trace of meat cooking down in the mess. The halls were alive with movement—soldiers coming off night rotations, runners ferrying supply crates, maintenance crews working the power conduits along the wall seams. It was a pulse. A rhythm she could feel beneath her boots.

Daryas adjusted the strap on her rifle as she moved, falling into pace with the corridor's steady flow. The training yard was already filling when she cut across the main hall, the first squads lining up for drills.

She rounded a corner and nearly collided with a crate—stacked chest high, teetering dangerously—and the kid behind it, who was struggling to keep the whole mess from toppling over.

The topmost box shifted. Cabbages—real ones, green and battered but fresh—tumbled out and hit the floor in a wet-sounding roll.

"Whoa, easy!" Daryas said, reaching out to steady the top crate before it collapsed completely.

The kid cursed under their breath—fast, sharp, and entirely unrepentant—as they scrambled after the runaway produce. Barely eleven or twelve, all wiry limbs and stubborn energy, with a shock of hair half falling into their eyes and a loose jacket tied half-on, half-off around their waist.

"Not my fault!" the girl said defensively, wrestling two of the rolling cabbages back into the crate. "They overloaded the carrier and then told me to 'hustle it over before first mess.' Like it's my fault half this junk's still got roots on it."

Daryas caught a cabbage with one foot before it rolled into the stairwell and nudged it back with a small smile. "You always talk this much?"

The girl grinned, flashing crooked teeth. "Only when I'm about to get blamed for something that isn't my fault."

Daryas chuckled under her breath and helped lift the crate back into better balance. "Where you headed?"

"Mess hall. They're short on prep hands again." The girl wiped a dirt-streaked hand across her forehead, smearing a line clean. "Some big official breakfast. Commander's briefing day or something."

Daryas stiffened just slightly, though she didn't show it.

"Commander?" she asked lightly.

The girl snorted. "Varek. Duh. Everyone talks about him like he's already running the place. Not that he's wrong for it."

Daryas tilted her head, amusement flickering behind her exhaustion. "You know him?"

"Know of him," the girl said, lifting her chin like it was obvious. "Everyone knows him. Even the runners."

The crate threatened to slip again, and the girl swore under her breath, hauling it up with a grunt.

"I'll walk you to mess," Daryas said, steadying the load with one hand.

The girl shot her a suspicious look. "You offering to carry it?"

"Not a chance."

That drew a laugh.

They moved together down the hall, the crate between them, the smell of dirt and fresh produce trailing after them as they blended into the living heartbeat of the stronghold.

Daryas didn't ask the girl's name. Not yet. It didn't matter here—not today. But there was something in the sharpness of her movements, the way she gritted her teeth without apology, that felt familiar in a way Daryas couldn't quite place.

They reached the mess hall without any more escaped cabbages.

The girl shot Daryas a quick grin, dropped the crate onto the intake counter with a theatrical thud, and bolted before one of the prep hands could rope her into another delivery. Daryas chuckled under her breath, watching the girl weave through the early morning crowd, disappearing into the low haze of kitchen steam and muttered orders.

It was early yet, but the mess was already filling. Lines of soldiers and trainees snaked between the tables, gear clattering softly as packs were dumped beside chairs and weapons were slung under the bench seats. The smell of ration stew thickened in the air—heavy with overcooked beans and the faint metallic tang of reconstituted protein—but it was still better than going hungry.

Daryas snagged a battered metal cup of weak coffee from the end of the serving line and drifted toward the quieter edges of the hall. She wasn't hungry, not really. The low churn of nerves that had settled in her gut before first light hadn't left her yet.

Training rotation would post in another half-hour.

Across the mess, a few other trainees from her cohort huddled together around a tabletop map, trading quiet commentary and half-hearted insults about the next round of drills. She recognized most of them—faces from the long march through rotations, the ones who hadn't washed out, the ones still standing.

Rika, towering over the others with that perpetual scowl carved into her brow. Darnel, who could shoot tighter groups than anyone under twenty but couldn't keep his mouth shut to save his life. A few newer faces she hadn't worked with much yet—eager, jumpy, still smoothing out the rough edges.

She caught Rika's eye across the room. The woman lifted her chin in a brief nod, a silent invitation, but Daryas shook her head lightly and turned away. Not yet. She needed a breath first. A step back to remember that not every fight had to be a sprint.

She found an empty seat near the east-facing window—one of the few places in the compound where the sun actually cut through the haze—and dropped into it, stretching her legs out until her boots tapped lightly against the chair across from her.

The coffee was bitter, nearly cold already, but she drank it anyway. It grounded her more than it warmed her.

She finished the last of the coffee and set the cup down carefully on the edge of the table; the metal scraping softly against the worn surface. Across the mess, the morning crowd thickened, soldiers and trainees filling the benches, some still laughing, some already lost in quiet conversation about rotations and loadouts.

Outside the window, the yard stretched wide and busy, a current of movement that never really stopped. The sun traced slow paths along the walkways, catching on the plates of moving figures, glinting off the barrels of rifles stacked near the depot doors. It wasn't a perfect place. It wasn't safe, not really. But it worked. It moved. It survived.

And so did she.

Daryas shifted her weight, pushing to her feet with a low roll of her shoulders as the last of the coffee settled into her system. Training drills would post soon, and she had no intention of being the last one to report. She slung her helmet under one arm, adjusted the rifle strap across her chest, and moved through the crowd without looking back.

The walk to the range cut across the southeast corridor, past the power bay and out through the open-sided corridor that bordered the shooting field. Stepping outside, the air immediately felt drier and cooler, a lingering chill from the recent night. The long field stretched ahead, lined with raised barriers, reactive targets, and shaded shooting posts spaced at precise intervals. Training banners hung limp in the low breeze, their colors faded under sun and repetition.

A few of the early squads had already posted up, checking weapons and prepping gear.

"Daryas," one of the instructors called as she passed. "Lane six. You're on long range today."

She gave a quick nod and turned toward the marked station. The mat had already been rolled out, and a rifle waited on the bracketed platform—standard issue, tuned for field accuracy, stripped of everything unnecessary. The familiarity of it settled into her muscles as she dropped into position, her hands already moving through the checks with a practiced rhythm. She didn't need to think anymore—adjust the bipod angle, calibrate the rangefinder, ease into the stock. Her body remembered what precision felt like.

In the lane beside her, someone else had already taken position. Not a face she recognized, but that wasn't unusual.

Rotation lists shifted constantly, and not everyone talked enough to make an impression.

He wore Vanguard trainee armor like hers, but the plates were a muted slate grey—distinct from the standard black most trainees were issued. It wasn't out of regulation, just unusual. Some squads ran color variants based on unit history or command structure, and whoever he trained under had enough pull to let it slide. The armor was clean, not factory-new but maintained, carrying the same edge she saw in the way he held himself—present, balanced, utterly focused.

His helmet sat clipped behind him, untouched. His hair was dark, a little long at the front, swept to one side where it met the brow, like he hadn't given it much thought but still somehow made it work. He was roughly her age—maybe a few months younger, maybe not. Young, but sharp. Everything about him suggested quiet competency, not the kind that needed to be seen, but the kind that didn't have to explain itself.

He didn't look at her.

Daryas slid into prone, adjusted her breathing, and fell into sync with the field.

"Station one," the instructor called from downrange. "Five rounds. Stationary targets. Three hundred meters. On my mark."

The command echoed in the space between them, and Daryas inhaled slowly, settling her cheek against the stock, the world narrowing to a tight window of scope glass and breath control. When the targets flickered into place, flat silhouettes outlined against the dry basin wall, she began to fire—measured, precise, calm. One after another. Her grouping held tight, just off-center by a finger's width, and the rifle's recoil settled into her shoulder like it belonged there.

Then she looked over.

His five were already marked. All dead center. The grouping was so close it nearly looked like a single impact.

He hadn't moved. He hadn't adjusted. He simply waited for the next call.

Daryas realigned her sightline and flexed the fingers of her support hand. It wasn't frustration, not exactly—just the first quiet ping of alertness. Something worth watching.

"Next drill. Moving targets. Variable speed and pattern. Fire on call."

She breathed in, released, and fired on rhythm. The targets darted in and out behind simulated cover, erratic but predictable if you knew how to time your lead. She tracked each with precision, dropping four clean, clipping one just off-center. Her cadence felt right. Her movements were smooth. It was a good run.

He didn't miss.

No reaction. No adjustment. He completed the drill like it was a walk. Clean. Effortless. Quiet.

Daryas didn't change her position, but her posture shifted— just slightly, shoulders resetting beneath the harness straps. Her fingers moved with more care now, every part of her honed down to match him beat for beat.

"Final set," the instructor called. "Five hundred meters. Wind shifting right. Adjust and fire."

The distance required a little more correction, and the heat rising off the ground began to ripple the outlines of the targets, just enough to blur judgment. She fired four rounds in solid sequence, but the fifth drifted—too far to be counted as clean.

His fired just before hers landed. No drift. Five rounds, each one snapping into the far metal plate with silent precision.

When the drill ended, Daryas pulled back from the scope slowly, her breath shallow from the length of the hold. She sat up, rested her elbows on her knees, and watched him stand.

He moved with the same unbothered control he'd held the whole time—slung the rifle over his shoulder, retrieved his helmet, and turned away from the line without even glancing in her direction.

But just before he stepped off the mat, he paused.

His hand reached up—not a wave, not a salute—just a subtle adjustment to the edge of his collar. Then he looked toward her, just for a breath, eyes calm and unreadable, not challenging but not dismissive either.

A flicker of recognition passed between them, not as people who knew each other, but as competitors who had just seen something worth remembering.

Then he walked away.

Daryas remained in place for a few seconds longer, watching the ripple of heat blur his shape as he crossed toward the far end of the range. She'd been outshot before, but never like that. Never by someone who didn't even need to try.

She didn't know his name. Didn't ask.

But something about that quiet, grey-armored trainee stayed with her as she packed her gear and walked off the line.

Chapter 7 – The Weight of Memory

The sun hung low against the stronghold's west ridge, stretching long shadows across the cracked training fields and coating everything in a wash of gold. The heat was beginning to break, but it still clung to the stone and steel like a second skin, the air heavy with the scent of sweat, scorched dust, and spent rounds.

Daryas rolled her shoulders back, wincing slightly at the pull in her spine. Her armor sat heavier than usual today, every strap and buckle pressing against sore muscle and bruised bone. The day's drills had gone long—ground rotations, grappling drills, full-field live fire. The kind of day where no one got out without a limp or a scrape or something worse.

She stayed after the others peeled away, letting the training grounds clear, cleaning her rifle with slow, methodical strokes. The weapon wasn't hers, not yet. Still technically on loan. But she knew it like she knew the rhythm of her breath. She knew what it meant to make something that wasn't yours feel like home.

She was wiping the last streak of carbon off the barrel when she heard footsteps behind her—measured, familiar. She didn't need to turn to know who it was.

"You know," Varek said, coming to stand beside her, "at some point, someone's going to start charging you rent for staying out here this late."

She straightened, slinging the rifle across her back as she glanced up at him. "You volunteering to file the paperwork?"

"Gods, no," he said, shaking his head. "You've seen what I do to forms."

They walked without speaking for a while, cutting across the lower yard toward the high overlook behind the training depot. The compound moved quietly around them, evening drills winding down, maintenance teams beginning their patrols. The sounds of work and routine filtered through the air like background hum—footfalls, clanking gear, the occasional barked order.

When they reached the top of the overlook stairs, they leaned together against the railing. The wind was higher here, catching at Daryas' braid and pushing the violet streak against her shoulder. Below them, the stronghold worked like a machine that refused to stop moving—livestock pens in rotation, security patrols rotating, two recruits running late to mess and getting chewed out by someone near the depot.

They stood that way for a while, not needing to say anything. They never had to fill silence.

Eventually, Varek spoke again, quieter this time. "You ever think about how far we've come?"

"Every day," Daryas said.

"You've changed a lot."

"You haven't," she said, glancing over.

He smiled faintly. "Still too serious?"

"Still not funny."

"I'm hilarious," he muttered.

They both watched the ridge for a few moments more, letting the quiet stretch naturally.

"I've been thinking," he said. "Probably too much. It happens when I'm up at night reviewing reports and pretending I'm still a field soldier."

"You'll always be a field soldier," Daryas said.

He nodded. "Maybe. But the job's changing. I'm changing with it. And... I don't want things to go unsaid."

That caught her attention.

Varek didn't do emotional declarations. He didn't need to. He showed his loyalty through action, steadiness, being the one who always came back from the mission. But tonight he was leaning into the weight of the moment with something more vulnerable behind it.

"I care about you," he said, not looking at her directly. "Not just because you're good. Not just because I see something in you that deserves more. I care about you."

Daryas didn't flinch. She didn't step away. She just listened.

"I know we've never talked about it," he continued, "and I know it never could've happened. Not with the roles we play. Not with the lives we lead. It wouldn't work. But I needed you to know it."

She didn't answer immediately.

When she did, her voice was soft but steady. "I know. And I care about you, too."

He looked at her then, and she met his eyes. "But you're right. It never could've worked."

"I know," he said, smiling lightly, not sad. "But I think part of me will always wonder."

"Part of me will always be grateful," she replied. "For the way you've looked out for me. For how you pulled me out of something I didn't think I could survive."

He nodded slowly. "That's never going to change."

"I didn't think it would," she said.

They didn't linger in the conversation. They let it rest between them, a truth shared without needing to carry more weight than it already did.

Varek turned and stepped toward a small crate tucked near the wall. He popped the latches and lifted the lid.

Daryas stepped closer as he pulled the armor free.

The chestplate gleamed in the soft light—Vanguard standard, full gear, black with reinforced joints and clean, molded lines. But it wasn't the black that caught her breath.

Threaded through the armor, subtle and deep, was a web of violet.

It traced the inside edge of the bracers, curled beneath the collarbone seams, wove a line down the outside of the spine plate like it had always been part of the design. Not a symbol. Not a flourish.

Just the memory, built into the armor itself.

She stepped forward, laying a hand across the chestplate, fingers brushing the cool line of violet stitched through the armor.

"You've had this waiting," she said.

Varek gave a small shrug. "I knew the day would come."

Daryas lifted the armor, piece by piece, locking it into place with careful hands. The plates molded against her body like they belonged there. Piece by piece, she slowly let the armor envelope her, like a new skin. When she straightened, she felt the weight settle into her frame—not just the armor, but everything she had carried to get here.

"You're Vanguard now," Varek said. "It's not a question anymore."

She flexed her fingers inside the gloves. The seams creaked once, then held.

"I was always Vanguard," she said. "The armor just finally caught up."

He smiled at that—genuine, proud.

"We move in a few weeks," he said. "New post, new structure. I'll be promoted before then."

She raised an eyebrow.

"Sub-Commander," he clarified. "They'll make it official. But you already knew that."

"I did," she said. "You were always the one they'd choose. I'm guessing there's more promotions soon in your future."

Varek rested his hand lightly on her shoulder for just a second. Then he stepped back.

"Report to squad assignment at 0600 tomorrow," he said. "I've already slotted your name."

"What if I had said no? Changed my mind?" she asked.

"I wasn't worried about that from you. You've been walking like it's yours for a while now," he said, turning toward the stairs.

Daryas stayed on the overlook a few moments longer. The armor hugged her like a second skin. The wind shifted and tugged her braid slightly across her shoulder, the violet streak brushing against the new gear.

Chapter 8 – The Gift of a Father

The stronghold buzzed with a restless energy, a pulse that traveled through the stone under Daryas' boots and echoed faintly against the metal braces bolted into the walls. The move was coming fast. Everyone could feel it. The air tasted like dust and heated steel, laced with the sharper scents of soldered wiring and fresh-sealed cargo crates.

Daryas walked the main thoroughfare, the weight of her new Vanguard armor steady across her shoulders, the faint violet weave along the bracers catching the low morning light. She moved through the current of motion without needing to announce herself—soldiers shifted instinctively to make room, work crews offering absent nods, a few younger recruits straightening unconsciously when she passed.

Near the loading dock, a maintenance chief barked orders to a team trying to muscle a generator onto a rig without the proper lift harness. The younger ones heaved and cursed under their breath, boots slipping against the grit-covered stone.

"Use your legs, not your damn spines!" the chief bellowed, then caught sight of Daryas. His tone shifted almost reflexively. "Vanguard."

Daryas gave a slight nod. "They'll get it up, eventually."

The chief grunted, a smirk tugging at one corner of his mouth. "If they don't break it first."

She moved on, the sounds of effort fading behind her.

Outside the barracks cluster, she passed a trio of supply runners rolling ration crates onto an open skid. One of the younger ones—maybe fifteen, if he was lucky—fumbled a crate as it tipped sideways. He muttered something sharp under his breath as it slipped through his hands and cracked open at the corner, vacuum-sealed packs tumbling into the dirt.

Daryas bent without hesitation, catching two of the packs before they slid farther across the ground. She tossed them lightly onto the pile and straightened, meeting the boy's wide-eyed stare.

"You'll want to tape that before first check," she said mildly.

He flushed bright red and nodded so fast his helmet slipped sideways. His friend elbowed him sharply, mouthing, idiot under his breath.

Daryas let a small, private smile ghost across her face as she kept walking.

The stronghold smelled different this morning. Not just dust and sweat, but something sharper underneath—oil and rubber, the burn of fuel lines running hot under overloaded engines. The smells of leaving. The smells of lifting everything that mattered and hoping it survived the next move.

At the edge of the drill field, a group of fresh trainees ran close-quarters drills, their movements sharp but still rough, still catching on the old mistakes that broke formations. An instructor stalked the perimeter, calling corrections with a voice like sandpaper. One of the trainees broke pattern and caught a solid knock to the shoulder for it, spinning slightly off-balance.

Daryas paused, watching them a moment. One of the trainers spotted her—recognized the Vanguard armor, the stance, the silent presence—and barked an extra-sharp order back to his squad, rallying their line tighter. They straightened unconsciously under her gaze.

Daryas didn't say anything. She didn't need to. They were still young enough to believe that someone watching made them stronger.

She turned and made her way toward the south corridor, where the civilian quarters sat tucked behind the storage sheds and the secondary water tank. The pathways narrowed here; the walls patched with mismatched plating and burn-scarred barriers, everything layered together across years of moves and rebuilds.

Children played in the alleys between stacked cargo crates, tossing a battered rubber ball between them. One of them—barely older than eight—stopped mid-throw when she caught sight of Daryas, her mouth opening slightly in surprise.

"Is she Vanguard?" the girl whispered to her friend, too loud to be private.

The boy she threw the ball to—grimy-faced, missing a front tooth—nodded with solemn certainty. "Yeah. You can tell by the armor."

"Look at the colors," the girl said, pointing at the faint glimmer of violet thread visible along Daryas' wrist.

Daryas caught their wide-eyed stares and offered a small nod as she passed. It was enough to set them giggling, the ball forgotten as they watched her walk away.

Not so long ago, she would've been the one staring.

The thought struck somewhere low in her chest—not regret, not grief exactly, but the quiet ache of knowing the gap between who she had been and who she had become would never close again.

She crossed the final supply lane, the stone path cracked and uneven, leading toward the civilian rows tucked deeper behind the main stronghold walls.

The smells shifted here—less oil and dust, more warm bread baking in portable ovens, damp stone where water lines leaked down old conduits. The air was cooler, softer, quieter.

Ahead, she could already see the door she was looking for—simple metal plating, slightly crooked on its hinges, propped open with a worn crate.

Her chest tightened slightly, an old, familiar tightness she thought she had outgrown.

She hadn't been here in too long.

Too many excuses. Too much training. And now the stronghold was pulling itself apart for yet another move. Another break in the storm signalled to everyone that it was time to see what lie beyond this valley's rim. She knew what it would be.

Another valley, more undead, and more chances to prove herself. To earn her own squad. Daryas rubbed her hand along a vein of purple that ran up her arm. Brit would have been proud of where she was now.

Daryas pulled the rifle strap tighter across her back, set her shoulders against the low pull of guilt, and crossed the last stretch of ground toward her father's door.

The door to her father's quarters creaked when she pushed it open, sticking slightly against the warped frame before giving way.

Inside, the room was almost painfully familiar. Narrow cot, battered footlocker, cracked water dispenser in the corner. It smelled like worn leather, oil, and the faint sharpness of cleaning solvent that never quite scrubbed the years from the walls.

He sat on the edge of the cot, elbows on his knees, staring at a spot on the floor that didn't seem particularly interesting. His hair had gone almost fully grey now, buzzed short in a way that made him look even harder around the edges. His frame was still thick through the shoulders, but he seemed smaller somehow, like the world had been quietly carving him down a little more every year.

He didn't look up immediately.

"Took you long enough," he said, voice dry as dust.

Daryas smirked, stepping inside and nudging the door shut with her boot. "I thought you liked the peace and quiet."

He snorted without looking at her. "Peace, maybe. Quiet gets old."

Daryas shifted slightly, tugging at the strap of her armor. "How have you been since Mom died?" she asked, the words slipping out before she could find something softer.

He let the question sit there, like it weighed more than he had the strength to lift. His hand rubbed absently at his knee. "Getting by," he said eventually, voice rougher than before. He glanced up at her, the line of his mouth tightening. "You weren't at the funeral."

Her stomach twisted. She looked away for a second, toward the crooked water unit in the corner. "Couldn't get away from training," she said, the excuse sounding thinner in the air than it had in her head.

"Training," he repeated, the word dry, almost hollow. He shook his head slowly, a breath rattling out of him. "Your mother deserved more than an empty chair."

She didn't argue. She didn't offer another excuse.

After a long moment, he shifted again, a low sound escaping him like the start of another reprimand. But when he looked at her, something softer cracked through the gruffness.

"Doesn't matter now," he muttered. "She'd have understood. Better than I do anyway."

The sadness in his eyes lingered a second longer before he brushed it away with a grunt and a small, rough shake of his head.

They let the silence settle again, the stronghold humming quietly around them.

"She was the one who could see further than her nose," he said. "Me? I just kept my head down and fought the fight in front of me. And now I sit here wondering if I spent too much time fighting and not enough looking around at what was worth saving."

"You saved what mattered," Daryas said.

He grunted. "Maybe. Maybe not. Just wish you'd had more than this life waiting for you."

Daryas met his gaze, steady and sure. "I wouldn't trade it. Not if it meant losing what you taught me."

He huffed, shook his head like he didn't quite believe her, but there was something in his eyes that softened, nonetheless.

She crossed the room and pulled the half-broken chair away from the wall, flipping it around to sit backwards on it, arms resting casually across the back. They sat that way for a minute, the stronghold noise bleeding in faintly through the thin walls— rigs rumbling, radios crackling, boots moving in steady rhythm.

"Looks like they're about ready to tear this place apart," he said, finally glancing up at her.

"They're getting faster," she agreed. "Think they're finally figuring out they can't build strongholds like they're supposed to last forever."

He huffed, dry amusement pulling at the corner of his mouth. "Takes some people longer to learn what doesn't hold."

She tipped her head, studying him quietly. The man who had taught her how to shoot, how to keep her center, how to patch up a broken fence post with nothing but grit and wire and bad words.

The man who hadn't always known how to say the things that mattered.

"How's the arm?" she asked, nodding toward the way he was rubbing at his shoulder.

"Still attached," he said, a faint grin slipping through. "That's more than I can say for some."

She chuckled low under her breath. "You planning to pull that card every time you get out of kitchen duty?"

"Wouldn't you?"

"Fair."

Another small silence settled between them, this one easier. The kind that comes from people who know they don't need to fill every space with sound.

He shifted slightly, wincing at the pull of his joints.

"I didn't expect to get this old," he said, voice quieter now, like it cost him something to admit it. "Didn't think I'd have to sit around watching the world move on without me."

Daryas leaned forward a little on the chair, resting her chin against her crossed arms. "You didn't sit. You fought. You kept us moving."

"Yeah," he said. "And somewhere along the way, I stopped seeing you."

That pulled her up short. For the first time in a long while, she found herself speechless.

He scrubbed a hand over his face, rough and unpolished. "I was so damn focused on keeping us alive that I didn't see who you were turning into. Didn't give you time to be anything else."

She didn't rush to answer. Let the words settle.

"I learned from the best," she said finally.

He chuckled again, soft and ragged. "Gods help you if that's true."

Outside, the stronghold pulsed and shifted—rigs moving gear, shouted orders blending into the constant mechanical hum of preparation. It should have felt urgent, pressing. But here, in this room, everything seemed to move slower.

He nodded toward the foot of the bed.

"Under there," he said gruffly. "Old chest. You'll want what's inside."

Daryas slid off the chair and knelt beside the bunk, the new Vanguard armor creaking slightly at the joints as she moved. She reached under and pulled out a battered metal case, the edges scuffed and worn from years of hard travel.

The latch fought her, stiff with grime, but it popped free after a moment.

Inside, wrapped in faded cloth, was the old Vanguard rifle— the one her father had picked up from a fallen soldier all those years ago when everything else had fallen apart. The grip was worn smooth in places. The casing scratched and scarred, but the faint pulse of the trexium core still glowed steady and warm beneath the surface.

She lifted it carefully, the weight of it settling into her arms like a memory.

He watched her, a line tightening along his jaw.

"Not much to look at," he said. "But it's the only thing that kept us breathing long enough to get you here all those years ago."

She turned the rifle over in her hands, fingers brushing across the battered casing.

"I thought you kept it for you," she said.

"I kept it for you," he said simply.

She closed the case carefully, pressing her palm flat against the lid for a breath before standing.

He shifted on the bed, grimacing at the effort.

"You deserved more than strongholds and scavenged rifles," he said, his voice rough again. "You deserved more than fights stacked on top of fights."

She tightened her grip on the case, feeling the weight settle deep into her chest.

"You gave me what you could," she said.

He smiled—a tired, lopsided thing that didn't quite reach his eyes.

"You gave yourself the rest," he said.

They sat in that small, battered room a little longer, the world rushing past outside without touching them.

Finally, he leaned back against the wall, pulling the blanket up higher over his knees.

"Go on," he said. "The world's not going to wait. I'm sure the mighty Vanguard teams need their hammer to find the right nail to hit."

Daryas stood, the case tucked under one arm, the armor shifting with her like a second skin. She crossed the threshold back into the sharp sunlight, the noise of the stronghold rushing up to meet her.

She didn't look back. Not because she didn't care but because she didn't think she could afford to.

Chapter 9 – Before They Were Angels

The war room felt smaller than usual, like the walls had shifted in overnight.

Heat bled off the old shield rigs tucked into the corners, the recycled air carrying the scent of burnt wiring, old metal, and a day's worth of sweat soaking into armor seals. Dust drifted in lazy curls through the filtered light from the overheads, catching on every breath, every shift of weight.

Daryas stood near the battered central table, helmet clipped against her thigh plate. Her armor moved with her like skin now—scuffed, worn, and steady. Around her, the squad settled into their usual orbit: Grassie, a steady hum of pent up energy at her left, arms folded and foot tapping once every few seconds against the cracked tile; Smokey, lounging against the far wall, half-shadowed, spinning a mag between two fingers like he had all the time in the world; Cab, newer, still in that tight, restless phase, bouncing lightly on her heels near the table's edge; and Rich, planted back against the far right wall, helmet sealed up tight like always, visor reflecting the faint shimmer of the tactical display.

Commander Hartwell stood at the front of the room, posture stiff, datapad loose in his gloved hand.

"Delta-Echo-Five deployed two days ago," Hartwell said, his voice cutting clean through the room's low hum. "Standard rotation. Minimal scavenger risk expected. Then comms cut. Scouts confirm survivors pinned in the main depot block. Civilian assets trapped inside. Raiders have fortified the outer yards."

He tapped the pad once, flicking up an overhead scan of the depot—half the perimeter fencing collapsed inward, dark scoring along the main road, the supply yards gutted and left to rot.

"We have a window," Hartwell said. "We move now, we get them out. If we wait—" he paused, gaze sweeping across them, "—we lose everyone."

Smokey's voice slid in from the back, casual but sharp. "What's the plan for insert? Flyers are still grounded after Zeta-Four, right?"

Hartwell's jaw tightened, but he nodded.

"No Vanguard flyers. Lost too many packs during the evacuation collapse. Ground-to-air sabotage."
He adjusted the pad. "That leaves rigs to the perimeter. One pass. No fallback."

Daryas shifted her weight slightly, feeling the vibrations from the engines humming through the floor even here.

Hartwell dropped the next words like they were nothing special.

"Skyhammer Maneuver."

Cab froze for a half-second, her gloved hands tightening on the edge of the table.
Grassie let out a slow breath through her nose, almost a sigh.

Daryas felt the tension snap tighter around them, pulling invisible lines between bodies that knew exactly how thin the margin was.

"No one's done a Skyhammer landing in the field in years," Cab said, voice a little too loud before she caught herself, swallowing hard. "We've all done the training, but—"

"It's too dangerous unless there's no other choice," Smokey finished for her, the usual edge of humor in his voice blunted to something heavier.

Hartwell simply nodded once. "There's no other choice."

Rich shifted his stance near the wall, the faint grind of boot against stone the only sign of movement.

"You realize if we don't land this perfectly," Grassie said, voice low and even, "we become the crater."

Daryas cut in without hesitation, her voice steady. "Then we don't do it wrong."

The room absorbed that in silence for a breath, the old lighting buzzing louder overhead.

Hartwell flicked the pad again, the depot's broken map reappearing.

"Targets inside are pinned under the admin block," he said. "Civilians mixed with wounded. Raider forces are controlling the west approach and the inner loading yards. East side partially collapsed—unstable. Watch for falling debris."

He tapped one corner of the map, highlighting a small cluster of signature pings.

"Intel shows at least thirty combatants still moving inside the walls. Maybe more."

Cab shifted again, fidgeting with the chinstrap of her helmet.

Hartwell's tone didn't change. "Expect dirty. Expect traps."

He tapped one final marker onto the overhead.

"And expect Kallan Brigg."

The name slid across the room like a dropped knife.

Smokey whistled low between his teeth. "Kallan 'One Shot' Brigg?"

Rich's visor tipped slightly in confusion. "Who?"

Daryas turned her head slightly toward him, catching a glint of light across the unbroken surface of his helmet.

"You don't know Brigg?" Smokey asked, half grinning like he couldn't believe it. "Old raider captain. Used to run hit-and-fades against Coalition scout posts. Supposedly took out a base commander with one shot from a half-broken hunting rifle during the fall at Grent's Crossing. That was without optics."

"Heard he once took down a supply rig with a pistol from a moving crawler," Grassie added, voice dry as desert stone.

"Probably half lies," Daryas said, but that wasn't the half that concerned her. It was the rest that were truths.

Even if the stories were inflated, they didn't make him less dangerous, especially cornered.

Hartwell folded the pad closed with a snap.

"You have twenty minutes. Get ready."

The loading bay rattled with noise.

Engines coughed and roared in cycles as crews hauled supply crates and landing gear into battered rigs lined along the perimeter gates. The air smelled of hot oil, charged battery packs, and the metallic tang of weapon lubricant baking under the midday heat.

Daryas adjusted the strap across her chest as she dropped down the stairs from the war room, boots hitting the cracked concrete hard. Her squad fell into place without needing to be called—Grassie moving with slow, deliberate steps, the butt of her rifle tapping lightly against her lower back; Rich ghosting along the edges of the group, head tilted slightly as he cross-checked the loadouts without removing his helmet; Cab jogging to catch up, helmet tucked under her arm, armor shifting loose where she hadn't tightened the straps properly yet; Smokey already waiting by the closest rig, leaning back against the cargo ramp like he had all the time in the world.

"You really believe that Brigg crap?" Rich asked over the squad comms, voice filtered into its usual low growl through his visor.

Smokey grinned, flipping his rifle upright with a lazy twist. "Guy's a walking cautionary tale. You screw around long enough, someone remembers your best shot and forgets the six times you missed."

"Sounds like someone's jealous," Cab muttered, fumbling with the clasp on her thigh rig.

Smokey slid his gaze sideways, all mock offense. "Jealous? Please. My worst day's cleaner than Brigg's best."

"Except for that time you got smoked in training," Grassie said mildly, stepping up to check the charge cells lining the side of their packs.

"Different circumstances," Smokey said without missing a beat. "I was operating under extreme tactical creativity."

Daryas let the back-and-forth roll through her without cutting it off. It wasn't just noise—it was pressure bleeding out; the squad finding their footing the way they always did when the ground underneath them started to crack.

She caught Cab tightening her gloves again, her hands moving faster than necessary.

Daryas stepped in without making a show of it, tapping two fingers lightly against the side of Cab's arm as she passed.

"You're ready," she said, voice low enough not to carry beyond them.

Cab drew a sharp breath in, nodded once, and tucked her chin down to check her boots like it was just another checklist item.

The rig doors ahead were swinging open now, the massive lift arms creaking under the strain. The carrier itself crouched low against the deck, its surface scarred with old blast marks and patch jobs welded into ugly plates.

No Vanguard flyers. No clean drops. Just steel and speed and bad odds.

Daryas pulled her rifle tighter against her chest, glancing across the yard to where the airship's boarding ramp lowered with a mechanical grind. The packs they'd strap to their backs—small, one-use burn packs designed to slow a freefall just enough to survive—were laid out in neat rows near the rig holds.

Grassie picked up two without comment, tossing one to Cab, who bobbled it against her chest before catching it properly.

Smokey caught Daryas' eye across the movement of crews strapping down med kits and emergency harnesses on the other ships destined for other missions. He arched one brow slightly, the smirk twitching at the edge of his mouth more felt than seen.

Daryas didn't return it outright. But she stepped closer as the squad gathered near the loading ramp, her shoulder pressing into his lightly through the armor—solid, real, grounding. His head leaned down and rested briefly on hers.

Neither of them said anything. Didn't need to.

The rig engines deepened into a steady growl, the deck plates vibrating underfoot as the main power feeds kicked through.

Cab finished locking the harness across her chest, face set now, knuckles white around the straps.

Rich ran another systems check from memory, murmuring low confirmations over the comms that only Grassie bothered to grunt responses to. The two of them were a funny pair. They worked well together. His bulk and her agility. Somehow, they made it work.

Daryas keyed the squad channel open.

"Final checks. Strap in tight. On my mark, we go."

The rig captain shouted boarding clearance across the open bay, his voice crackling over the rough speaker. Outside, the horizon shivered under the heat haze, Delta-Echo-Five's broken outline crouching low against the earth like a wounded animal waiting for the killing blow.

Daryas moved to the ramp first, her boots thudding solidly against the steel, the others slotting in around her without pause.

Smokey fell into line at her right, Grassie at her left, Cab and Rich tightening the formation at the rear.

They sealed the hatch behind them with the low grind of old hydraulics.

Inside the carrier, the light dimmed to a low emergency red, casting hard angles across their faces, sharpening the lines of old scars and new fears not yet spoken out loud.

Daryas rolled her shoulders back once, feeling the pack straps creak against her armor.

Skyhammer.

One drop.

One chance.

No way back.

She curled her hand into a loose fist against her thigh, letting the hum of the engines and the slow, heavy breath of her squad fill the silence.

No speeches, no drama. Just survival. The kind of faith that didn't come from prayers. Only from the trust you earned in the spaces between violence.

The rig jerked once, hard, as the engines kicked into full thrust. The deck rattled under their boots, and the world outside blurred into light and dust and the savage promise of the drop to come.

Chapter 10 – The War Angels

The rig shuddered again under her boots, a rough, guttural vibration that climbed through the deck plates and settled somewhere deep in Daryas' chest.

She sat braced near the rear hatch, the battered rifle case resting against her thighs, the whine of the engines growing sharper as they pushed harder into acceleration. The interior was bathed in low emergency red, throwing hard shadows across the squad as they finished their final gear checks.

Grassie sat cross-legged near the forward bulkhead, rolling her shoulders in slow circles to loosen them, the motion steady, almost lazy if you didn't know better.

Rich hunched low over his landing harness. Every strap and latch checked twice, moving with the mechanical precision of a man who didn't leave things to luck. His visor caught the low light, a reflection that masked whatever lay behind it.

Cab sat stiffly a few feet away, cradling her helmet in her lap, her fingers tapping a frantic, uneven rhythm against the hard shell before she caught herself and clenched them tight.

Smokey leaned against the cargo frame opposite Daryas, his rifle balanced loosely across his lap, his fingers tapping a slow beat against the side rail. His helmet sat beside him, his face bare and calm, the familiar lazy smirk tugging half-heartedly at his mouth as if, even now, he refused to let the tension own him.

Daryas exhaled slowly, rolling her shoulders back against the hard edge of the rig. She unlatched the rifle case and eased it open, her fingers moving with quiet familiarity. Inside, wrapped in worn cloth and old carbon burns, rested the trexium core from her father's rifle. A faint pink glow still pulsed from its heart— small, steady, warm like a hand pressed against her own.

She turned it slowly in her palm, feeling the minute vibrations humming through the casing. A breath caught in her chest, small and sharp. Across the rig, Smokey shifted, stepping forward into the narrow aisle between them. He didn't say anything.

He just knelt in front of her, one hand braced against the deck, and enclosed her hand—the core trapped between their palms—in a quiet, solid pressure. The touch was brief, a grounding more than a gesture. A silent promise that when they hit the ground, they would do it the way they always had.

Daryas opened her fingers around the core as Smokey pulled away, standing with the fluidity of someone who already knew what came next. She slipped the core into an ammo slot on her armor that she had modified to hold the older design.

The rig captain's voice crackled over the intercom, distorted by static and speed.

"Approaching drop zone. Ten seconds. Skyhammer green."

Daryas rose, slinging her rifle across her back, feeling the weight of it settle into the grooves worn into her body over a hundred missions.

Grassie finished a final tug on Cab's landing straps, tapping her shoulder once in silent reassurance.

Rich locked down his weapon harness, rolling his shoulders forward with a mechanical click of his joints.

Smokey popped his helmet on with one hand, the seals hissing closed with a soft exhale of pressure.

The ramp ahead groaned as it dropped into the rushing wind, the world outside a blurred maelstrom of dust and broken sunlight.

Beyond it, Delta-Echo-Five sprawled broken and bleeding against the horizon—walls sagging inward, smoke trailing lazy arcs into the pale sky, barricades shredded and abandoned across the loading yards.

Daryas keyed her squad channel, her voice low but carrying.

"Mark your burns. Land tight. Watch your flanks. Let's get our people and teach these scavengers what happens when they mess with the wrong people."

The world jerked again under the rig as the engines bellowed against the shifting weight.

The signal light above the hatch flashed from red to amber.

Cab sucked in a breath beside her.

Grassie shifted her center of mass, her fingers flexing once and going still.

Rich glanced up, then nodded once, sharp and certain.

Smokey tapped the butt of his rifle lightly against his armor in a silent beat.

The signal snapped green.

The rush of air hit her like a wall, stripping thought away, leaving only instinct.

The rig dropped from beneath her boots, the world tilting into a scream of wind and grit and sun-bleached light. She tucked her arms close, legs locked tight, diving through the sky like a falling blade.

The depot below surged up toward her, fractured buildings casting long skeletal shadows across the wreckage. Raiders scrambled across broken terrain, some firing blindly upward, others trying to rally under the sudden, impossible storm falling on them.

Trexium rounds blazed through the air around her—streaks of burning pink fire slicing long contrails through the dust, sizzling past her visor so close she could feel the heat of them through the armor seals.

Tracer lines stitched the sky below, crude and erratic, cutting the distance between life and death thinner than a breath.

Her HUD flashed altitude warnings, the numbers bleeding downward too fast.

Fifty meters.

Thirty.

Twenty.

The landing pack buckled against her back, burning compressed thrust into the fall. She waited until the last possible heartbeat—

Fired.

The thrusters slammed her upright in a brutal wrench; the air ripping at her limbs as she bled speed in a violent, gutting scream of force.

She hit the ground hard, knees bending to catch the impact, boots skidding across the cracked asphalt before she forced herself upright.

Around her, the squad landed—

Grassie dropped heavy into cover behind a shattered supply crate.

Rich rolled into a crouch against a broken light post, already leveling his rifle.

Cab stumbled, caught herself, and ducked low behind a scorched vehicle hull.

Smokey slammed down just ahead, rolling to a knee, his rifle already tracking targets.

The depot exploded into noise—gunfire, shouting, the whine of old generators kicking back to life to power defenses, and the sharp, screaming hiss of more trexium rounds burning through the shattered sky.

Daryas locked her rifle tight against her shoulder, feeling the hard, grounding pulse of the old core case tucked against her ribs. This was what she lived for.

The depot exploded around them the second their boots hit dirt.

Trexium rounds tore through the haze, leaving long, hissing scars of pink light that snapped past broken barricades and crumbling walls. Daryas hit the ground hard, boots digging into the cracked asphalt, rifle snapping up even as she moved forward. The squad surged into motion like pieces of a machine they'd spent years building.

Rich moved heavy on her right, the thick plates of his armor absorbing impacts as he braced into the shattered remains of a cargo loader, rifle barked deep and controlled, anchoring the line without needing to be told.

Grassie disappeared to her left, slipping low and fast through the gaps between broken crates and twisted debris, too quick to track, popping raiders with short, surgical bursts that hit before the enemy even realized she was there.

Cab darted wide, a flash of armor and grit, rolling over cover and crashing into the flank with wild energy—one, two raiders dropping before they even leveled their rifles.

Smokey stayed fluid on the edges, rifle tight to his shoulder, pink beams slicing through gaps in the barricades, picking off threats with unnerving precision. His shots burned the air, sizzling arcs threading the chaos with clean, lethal lines.

Daryas drove straight through the center.

Her rifle kicked against her shoulder in steady bursts—short, vicious exhalations of pink fire that cut through the first two raiders trying to scramble behind a supply stack. She advanced without hesitation, boots crunching over broken glass and spent rounds, the violet seams along her armor catching in the flickering light like ghost trails.

Five down inside the first minute.

Ten by the time they pushed clear of the outer yard.

Twelve bodies strewn across the wreckage as they carved forward into the bleeding heart of Delta-Echo-Five.

The squad moved by instinct, no need for shouted commands.

When Grassie dropped low behind a burned-out vehicle, Rich covered her without breaking stride.

When Cab broke right, sliding between cover, Smokey shifted fire automatically to clear her lane.

They had fought this dance countless times in training and in the field. They knew it well.

The raiders broke around them in ragged lines—scrambling for higher ground, shouting to cover their retreat—but Darya's Vanguards drove them like a fin splitting water.

Trexium rounds stitched the air above the courtyard, hissing and crackling through the dust clouds thickening around the depot walls.

Somewhere beyond the inner barricades, Daryas caught a flash of movement—civilians pinned under the wreckage of a collapsed loading dock, huddled low behind overturned pallets and twisted girders. Raiders had them boxed in, firing from raised scaffolding and broken second-level walkways, trying to herd them deeper into the kill zone.

Daryas pivoted low behind a sheared wall, scanning fast.

There—secondary objective.

She keyed the squad channel short and sharp.

"Secondary group located. Northeast quadrant."

Grassie answered first, voice clipped. "Acknowledged. Holding outer yard."

Rich shifted, voice calm and solid over the comms. "Anchor left. Covering your push."

Smokey's voice followed, dry and amused even now. "You're gonna owe me coffee if you get yourself killed."

Daryas gave a short grunt that passed for a smile and peeled off, trusting them to hold the ground behind her.

She sprinted low across open wreckage, weaving through smoking barricades and broken beams, the heavy bulk of the depot wall rising like a broken mountain ahead of her.

Gunfire stitched the air overhead, bullets sparking off stone and tearing through the brittle frames of abandoned gear. She ducked low, moving fast, cutting across the kill zone toward the pinned civilians.

In the distance, a heavier figure emerged from the smoke— armor scavenged and reinforced with old Coalition plates, rifle slung heavy across one shoulder, a curved machete glinting dark in his other hand.

Kallan "One Shot" Brigg.

Even through the dust and chaos, Daryas could feel the shift in the battle lines—like the air itself tightened around him.

She pressed forward without hesitating, her boots slamming into broken stone as she tore through the last choke point between her squad and the pinned civilians. Trexium rounds cut bright arcs through the murk, sizzling pink fire that slashed past crumbling barricades and shattered scaffold frames.

Daryas moved like muscle memory—two shots left, one quick turn, another raider down—clearing the path without thought, her armor vibrating with every impact and near-miss.

The civilians scrambled where she herded them, wide-eyed and ragged, clutching injuries and dragging each other up the shattered slope of a collapsed fuel depot. Daryas barked short, sharp commands, not stopping to see if they hesitated—pushing them higher, over jagged metal and broken girders, away from the killing floor.

Her rifle bucked against her shoulder, the targeting display flashing in sharp, angry bursts across her HUD.
Damage detected.
Trexium leak detected.

The next shot fizzled weaker, the beam sputtering as it cut through the air, a hiss instead of a crack.

She ducked a wild swing from a raider clutching a scrap-iron pike, rolling into cover and searching for a fresh mag to put into the housing—but the warning stayed she was out of fresh mags. The core she had was bleeding energy; the casing cracked somewhere deep in the rifle's frame.

No time to fix it.

She shoved the civilians forward, helping the last one—a boy barely old enough to hold a pistol—up and over a pile of debris.

"Stay low," she snapped, voice tight through the comm. "Stay behind cover. Move only when I say."

She pivoted to cover their backs—

And froze.

Across the debris-strewn courtyard, Smokey was locked in brutal hand-to-hand against a broad, scarred figure clad in a patchwork of Coalition armor and scavenged gear.

Even at a distance, Daryas could see the smile splitting Brigg's face—wide, cruel, hungry for the kill.

Smokey moved fast—his blade flashing in tight arcs, dodging brutal swings—but Brigg fought like a bludgeon, smashing Smokey back with sheer mass and feral precision.

The squad was pinned—Grassie trading shots across the loading ramp, Cab and Rich trying to punch through a fallback position—but too far to intervene.

Daryas lifted her rifle automatically, sighting Brigg through the dust—

The rifle clicked dry.

She yanked the core casing, but the diagnostics screamed empty.

The trexium core was drained. Nothing left.

Below, Brigg slammed Smokey hard into a pile of broken crates, disarming him with a wrench of brute force. Smokey staggered, knife flying from his hand, blood streaming down his temple.

Brigg's grin widened. He drew the machete slow, almost lovingly, the edge glinting red against the smoke.

"I've heard about you," Brigg said, voice carrying even over the chaos. "Best shot in the Vanguard, they say."

Smokey spat blood into the dust but didn't answer.

Brigg pressed the flat of the blade against Smokey's cheek, tilting his head roughly to the side.

"Let's see how sharp that eye really is."

Daryas' hands moved before she fully thought.

She snapped open the small side pouch on her belt, fingers closing around the battered, familiar weight—the old trexium core from her father's rifle. It still pulsed faintly against her skin, a small, stubborn glow, a memory pressed into metal.

It was the old design. But all rifles could fit the old cores.

Her fingers moved fast, flipping the casing latch, slamming the core into place.

The HUD flickered once, uncertain—

Then stabilized, power low but enough.

She lifted the rifle again, sighting through the fractured lens, breath steady against the rising burn in her lungs.

Smokey struggled under Brigg's grip, trying to twist free—but Brigg pressed the blade tighter against Smokey's brow, the first bead of blood welling just below the eye.

Daryas squeezed the trigger.

The old core roared once—pure, burning pink—and the shot tore through the air like a comet.

The beam struck Brigg clean through the temple, snapping his head sideways before the rest of his body even realized it was dead.

He dropped in a heap, machete clattering against the broken concrete.

For a second, the courtyard held still—the smoke curling in slow spirals above the wreckage, the dust hanging heavy in the choking light.

Daryas lowered her rifle slowly, the casing burning against her gloves.

Across the field, Smokey slumped to his knees, one hand pressed against the side of his bloodied face, but alive.

The old core sputtered one last flicker of pink against her HUD—

—and went dark. The transport bay was quiet except for the soft whine of cooling engines and the low murmur of medical crews moving between stretchers.

Delta-Echo-Five loomed behind them in the dying light, smoke rising from the broken walls like the last breath of something too stubborn to fall cleanly. The civilians huddled in small groups near the medical rigs, battered but alive, eyes flicking constantly toward the squad without knowing where to look.

Daryas stood with her rifle slung against her chest, the battered case holding her father's core tucked tight at her hip. Her armor was scorched in places, cracked along the forearms and thighs where the worst of the landing had bitten deep. She barely felt it. Not yet.

The squad formed a loose half-circle around the rear loading ramp.

Grassie wiped a blood-smeared hand across her faceplate, helmet tucked under one arm. Her braid was half-torn loose, dust coating the strands.

Rich leaned against the rig wall, still helmeted, arms folded, his rifle resting lightly across his chest. No words, just watching.

Cab sat on a supply crate a few meters away, one arm draped across her lap, helmet dangling from her fingers, a split across the bridge of her nose leaking a slow trickle of blood.

Smokey stood nearby, half-shadowed by the frame of the rig, his face still bloodied, the wound across his right eye raw and stitched hastily in the field. His good eye tracked Daryas as she moved, quiet and steady; a thread of something unspoken stretched between them.

Commander Hartwell crossed the open path in the middle of the makeshift landing area with long, purposeful strides, his soldiers armor still dusted white with ash from the courtyard fires. He stopped a few paces from the squad, hands on his belt, helmet tucked under one arm.

He studied them for a long moment.

"You pulled them out," Hartwell said finally, voice low and rough. "All of them."

He turned his gaze toward the civilians for a breath, then back to them.

"You hit that yard like an airstrike," he said. "Fast. Brutal."

He shook his head once, a sharp, approving motion.

"Like an air strike from heaven."

The words hung in the thick air, heavier than anything else that had passed between them.

Hartwell pivoted away without another word, striding back toward the command line, shouting final orders to the med teams.

The squad stayed where they were, not moving, not speaking.

Daryas reached down and tightened her glove around the worn strap of her rifle, feeling the old warmth of the battered, now spent core still pressed close to her side.

Smokey caught her eye across the gathering dusk. Gave her the smallest nod. She returned it, slow and sure.

The world had shifted around them while they fought.

And when the smoke cleared, their reputation remained. They had fallen like a hammer from heaven against their enemies. Like angels, made for a singular purpose.

They were the War Angels.

Over the Fire

The night was cold on the ridge.

The fire crackled low in the hollow between two outcroppings of stone, sending thin ribbons of smoke twisting up into a sky heavy with stars. Wind moved lazily through the rocks, carrying the dry scents of ash, old blood, and the scorched earth that still bled from the long battles they had left behind.

Below them, the stronghold slept—its shield towers buzzing faintly against the broken skyline; the walls patched with the scars of too many sieges. Beyond that, under the slivered moons, the shattered wreckage of the Purge ship stretched like the ribs of some ancient beast, twisted and silvered in the low light.

Miner sat with his back against a battered slab of stone, a dented mug cooling slowly between his hands. Around the fire, the survivors sprawled without ceremony—armor dusted with soot, movements slower than usual, weariness buried deep under the easy posture of people who had fought too hard to pretend they weren't still standing.

The proximity sensors blinked a steady blue perimeter around them. No alarms. No threats. Just a quiet so deep it seemed to settle into the bones.

Daryas sat across the flames. Her shoulders slouched in a way that said she hadn't quite decided if she trusted the silence yet. Grassie picked at the strap of her boot with the tip of a combat knife, her braid loose over one shoulder, boots planted solid against the stone.
Cab leaned back against a crate, legs sprawled out, one hand idly tossing pebbles at the fire and missing half the time.

Rich stood a little apart, as he always did, arms crossed over his chest, his helmet sealed tight, the reflection of the firelight dancing across the smooth curve of his visor.

And the space between them where Smokey would have been sat heavy, a quiet that none of them pointed at, but none of them ignored.

Miner let the silence stretch for a while, the fire popping and hissing as the wood shifted.

"So," he said eventually, breaking it with the low scrape of his voice, "that's how you got the name."

Daryas smiled—small, tired—but there was a warmth under it as she tipped her head back to stare at the stars.

"Yeah," she said in a nonchalant. "Basically."

There was a beat of quiet.

Then Cab snorted and flicked another pebble into the flames.

"Basically?" she echoed. "You left out, like, ninety percent of it."

Grassie laughed under her breath, low and rough. "Didn't even mention the time Smokey tried to drive us off a cliff."

"Or the time I put grease on Grassie's boots so she couldn't even stand during gear up that time we fought the other stronghold," Cab added, tossing another pebble, this one catching a spark and sending it dancing up into the night.

Across the fire, Rich shifted, the movement subtle but deliberate.

For a second, Miner thought that was all.

But then, with a slow, deliberate motion, Rich reached up and unclasped his helmet, the seals hissing softly as he twisted it free.

He pulled it off and tucked it under his arm, standing there bareheaded for the first time Miner could remember.

His hair was deep black, short at the sides but long enough to fall forward across his forehead. His skin was darker than Miner had pictured under the armor, marked with faint old scars that said more about his life than any words ever had. His eyes, dark and steady, caught the firelight and reflected it back not in anger, not in grief—but in something quieter.Dark and steady, his eyes caught the firelight, their reflection showing not anger or grief, but something quieter. Something unbreakable.

The rest of the squad went still for a moment, the fire crackling louder in the silence.

Daryas just smiled wider, slow and real.

"Rich," Cab said, mock whispering behind one hand, "has a face. Who knew?"

Grassie chuckled, low and deep. "Told you he wasn't a ghost under there."

Rich just shrugged like it didn't matter, stepping closer to the fire, letting the heat brush against his armor.

"You told the big strokes," he said, voice steady, quiet. "But you left out too much."

Daryas tipped her head, lazy defiance sparking behind her tired smile. "Told the parts that mattered."

Rich tilted his head slightly, the fire catching the edges of his scarred cheek.

"All of it matters," he said. "If we're telling it... we tell it right."

He crouched down near the fire, setting his helmet carefully beside him, and leaned forward, elbows resting against his knees.

He looked across the flames—at Daryas, at Grassie, at Cab—and for a second, it was like the war against the Architects they had found themselves embroiled in hadn't stolen anything yet.

Then he began to speak, voice low, weaving the beginning of the real story—the one that he had lived, not just survived.

The fire crackled higher, and the wind carried the words up into the stars.

www.ingramcontent.com/pod-product-compliance
Lightning Source LLC
Chambersburg PA
CBHW071541100726
47908CB00004B/1456